RYLAND

The Golden Streak Series
Book 1

By

Kathi S. Barton

World Castle Publishing, LLC

WCP

World Castle Publishing, LLC
Pensacola, Florida

Copyright © Kathi S. Barton 2013
ISBN: 9781939865328
First Edition World Castle Publishing, LLC May 5, 2013
http://www.worldcastlepublishing.com

Licensing Notes

Cover: Karen Fuller
Editor: Brieanna Robertson
Editor: Maxine Bringenberg

CHAPTER 1

"Where's your secretary?"

Ryland shrugged at his brother.

"She does know that it's important that she stay at her desk and answer the phone, right?"

"Where is yours? Under the desk again? I heard that she spends a great deal of time there." Ryland had no time and less energy to deal with Alistair right now, and there was a waning moon in a few days as well. "You should mind your own business and let me—"

"Yours quit yesterday. And mine is at her desk doing her job."

Ryland looked at his brother, trying to decide if he was jerking his chain or not.

"She handed in her resignation two weeks ago. Yesterday was her last day. I take it you didn't throw her a going away party."

"How do you know that's what happened? Maybe she simply took a couple of weeks off. She couldn't have any vacation time saved. She's only been here what? A couple of months?" Ryland realized he didn't even know her name. When a sheet of paper flew across his desk at him, he picked it up.

Her name was Colette Bridges and she'd left with notice stating that she'd found a less stressful job. She'd gone on to say that working for Ryland Golden was akin to working for a dictator, and she wished him luck finding someone else. Ryland tossed the page back at Alistair.

"You have any idea what she's talking about?"

Ryland flushed at his question.

"If you keep this up, no one will work for you no matter what we pay them. I didn't think that I'd have any luck finding you someone as it was."

"Did you?" Alistair nodded. "When does she start? Never mind, I don't want her. I want a male to work for me. Women are too emotional and think things should be handed to them with a pretty bow. I fucking don't have time for bows or emotions."

"You said it, not me." Alistair stood up. "Too late for this girl. She starts in the morning. But I will look for someone else. I don't think you and this girl will suit either, but she owes me her fee and this was a way to get what I charged her. And Ryland, don't bite her. She will bite you back."

"You mean you hired me a criminal to answer my phones? Great. Will I need to carry my gun just so she doesn't murder me in my own office?" Ryland flushed again, his face so hot he wanted to turn away from Alistair.

"You are such a charmer it's small wonder that you don't have a mate and ten kids by now." Alistair walked to the door, but turned before exiting. "Her name is Miss Lawrence. Try and make it through the week with her until I can get you someone else."

After Alistair left, Ryland walked to his bathroom and splashed cold water on his face. His cat was pissy because he'd not been on a run in…he couldn't remember the last time. But Ryland had to be stern. No one else in the family had the balls to do what he did daily and still live with themselves. He walked back to his desk and looked over the proposal that had been a pain in his side since the previous month.

The building was going to make them millions. Ryland knew his mother would say that they had enough money, that he needed to relax and see the area right outside his office building, but things were coming to a head and he wanted to finish them. He frowned, knowing that he'd said that about the last project and the two before that. Ryland liked working hard, and long hours…it was what he lived for.

Ryland looked up when his mom walked into his office.

"Have you found a replacement for Colette yet?" She sat in the chair across from him. "Poor girl had a hard time of it, and I had to work hard to get her to stay for as long as she did."

"You knew she was leaving?"

She nodded and played with the button on her jacket.

"Why the hell didn't you say something to me? I thought she'd gone to lunch early."

She raised her brow at him and he knew he'd gone too far with her. She was his mom and he loved her dearly, but she scared the shit out of him most of the time. When she continued to look at him with that mom look, he sat up in his chair. "I'm sorry. Alistair said he found someone to replace her for this week. I think he's looking to find me someone else. A male someone else. Women and I don't see eye to eye when it comes to work ethics."

"Oh, Ryland, you and women don't see eye to eye on any level. When was the last time you went out with a real girl?" He asked her what that was supposed to mean. "It means one that you've known for more than the time it takes you to get her undressed. And as cranky as you seem to be all the time, I'm thinking that doesn't happen often enough either."

"This is not a conversation I'm comfortable having with my mother. Drop it or I'll leave. I can work just as well from my hotel room as I can from here."

"Who does that? What kind of person who has all the money he could ever hope to spend lives in a hotel room? You should have a house. A place where you can run in the trees with someone. Buy one if only for the investment. You're too old to have room service pick up after you daily and make your bed." She stood up. "I'm going to find you one if you don't. I'm serious about this, Ryland. Get a girlfriend, and not from a bar, and buy a home for yourself. Maybe then you'll find someone to settle down with and marry."

"I'm not in the mood for this bashing of Ryland crap. And you will not buy me a house. If I wanted one, I'd find it for myself." She paused at the door and looked back at him. "Thank you, but I'm capable of finding my own way."

"Perhaps you misunderstood me. I didn't ask you if I could. I said you will or I will. You have until the end of the moon pull to put a bid on one, and have it purchased by the middle of next month or so help me, I'll do it for you. And you will not like my idea of a house."

She was out the door before he could say anything else. He wasn't really sure what he'd have said to her, but he would have thought of something to get himself into deeper shit with her. Looking at the calendar, he realized she'd only given him eleven days to look. *Sweet of her*, he thought as he stretched out his neck to ease the tension. He did not need this.

Working through lunch, he was ready to get out at almost nine that evening. He was starving, and decided to pick up a

8

sandwich from the deli and take it to the hotel with him. He was riding up to the penthouse when he remembered the girl was starting tomorrow.

"Mother fuck," he muttered to himself as he tossed his coat and briefcase on the sofa. Taking his dinner to the kitchenette, he put everything on a paper plate and took it to the table/office that he had set up there. Eating while working, he finally went to bed at midnight. He'd done all he could with the proposal, and now it was up to the seller.

~~~

"Is that what you're wearing?"

Bronwyn looked down at her pants and shirt.

"You can't be serious."

"I am, and I am. What's wrong with this? It's clean. And he told me to dress like I did in the courtroom. This is what I wore every day." She'd had to rinse it out nightly, but she had worn it. She looked at her roommate and friend, Sindy Wilson.

"How much time do I have? Never mind, you wouldn't wait if I had ten years. Just let me give you a blouse. Wearing a man's shirt to work is not good. Where are you working anyway?" Sindy walked out of the room before Bronwyn could answer, and was back in less time than it took Bronwyn to get her jacket on. She, of course, tisked at that as well.

"You can just take that back. First of all, it won't fit me. I'm a tad bit bigger than you across the boobs, and, secondly, I cannot...no, I won't wear yellow. I look like someone drained me."

"You're right, it does wash you out completely. I've never met a woman who had less fashion sense than you do. Don't you own anything that's feminine?"

Bronwyn huffed at her.

9

"Okay, but at least wear this. It's blue like everything else you own, so it'll go with all your shirts. You do know that there are other fabrics beside cotton, right?"

Bronwyn pulled on the jacket and wasn't surprised to find that it wouldn't button. Without pointing this out to Sindy, she took it off, pulled her hoodie back on, and went to the door. She was nearly through it when Sindy said her name.

"You never did tell me where you're working and for who. That guy, your attorney, he's yummy. If he can find me a job working...undercover, I'd work for him for free."

"I'm working at the Golden Towers. Mr. Golden said that his family owns it and that I would be in some sort of pool until I paid him off. It should take me about four hundred years."

Sindy whistled. "Christ, B, that's big league stuff, working for the Goldens. I should have made you buy new clothes."

Then she'd owe her too. Going to the elevator, Bronwyn pushed the button. Nothing. Knowing that it was out again, she went to the stairwell to walk down the ten flights. She supposed she should have been glad she wasn't in it again when it went down. Two hours closed up in that thing last winter had nearly made her a frozen Popsicle. She was out of the building ten minutes behind schedule.

By the time she got off the bus in front of the Golden Towers she wasn't as early as she'd meant to be. Her workday was supposed to start at nine, and she had wanted to be there at eight. But the elevator and a broken down bus had her going inside at eight-thirty. She rushed to the security desk, knowing that they were going to hold her up even more.

"I'm Bronwyn Lawrence. I'm supposed to start today." The man picked up his clipboard as she continued. "I'm probably not on the list. I just spoke to Mr. Golden yesterday and he said that he'd fix it so I could work." She realized she was babbling and snapped her mouth closed. The man winked at her and she was suddenly unsure of herself. No one winked at her.

"You're right here, miss. Come this way and I'll set you up with a badge and parking spot." She told him she didn't drive, but followed. "You'll need to see Mr. Golden about a car then. He will require you to have one. Do you have a driver's license?"

"Yes. But I don't need a car. This is only for a little while until I can get something better." She flushed when he looked at her. "I mean one that I don't have to come clear across town to get to. I suppose this is a good place to work, but I—" She shut her mouth again. She hated that she babbled when she was nervous. And she was, very much so.

Bronwyn followed him to the office and sat when he asked her to. She was to have her picture identification taken, and then she'd be escorted upstairs by him. He told her his name was Stan Flores.

"Which Golden are you working for?"

Bronwyn waited until he snapped her picture before answering. She told him she was just in the work pool. He looked at her oddly, but didn't comment. At a quarter till nine they were headed upstairs. "You'll be trained today by Liz Baker. Liz is really nice and has a wonderful attitude about life in general. She'll be able to help you get over this first day and, after that, I'm betting you'll be fine." The doors opened, and she saw a single desk and a lovely office. "Liz will be right up."

The doors closed and she sat down in one of the chairs against the wall. She was still sitting there when a man came in and went into the office doors in front of her at just a little after nine. The phone started ringing about two minutes later.

At nine-thirty she couldn't take it anymore. The phone had never stopped ringing, and she was sure she'd been forgotten about. Going to the phone, she picked it up while digging through her purse for a pen and something to write on.

"Golden Towers." She didn't give her name because she was sure she wasn't supposed to be answering the phone. "How can I help you?"

"Is he in his office?"

She hesitated.

"Never mind. Tell him to get his ass to the meeting or I'll come there and kick his ass." The man hung up. She wrote down what he'd said, and the time, then saw that the phone number had come up on the ID, so she wrote that down as well. Before she could finish that note, another call came in. This went on for nearly two hours before someone came off the elevator. She looked at the woman there as she answered the phone.

"Golden Towers."

The woman sat down in the seat across from her and smiled. Bronwyn smiled back, but was looking for another corner to write on when the woman handed her a small pad of paper.

"Did you give him my message?" She looked at the thirty-three notes in front of her and told the man she'd not seen anyone. "He was supposed to be at this meeting when it started. We're now having lunch and he's still not here. Tell him that I sent Mom to haul his ass up here, and she won't be happy when she gets there."

"Yes sir." She hung up and looked at the woman. "I don't suppose you're Liz Baker, are you?"

"No. I'm Sandra Golden. You would be the new secretary, I take it?"

Bronwyn shook her head.

"Well, you could have fooled me. How long have you been here, Miss...?"

"Lawrence, Bronwyn Lawrence. Around eight forty-five. Ms. Baker was supposed to come and train me for the work pool. I haven't seen her, unless she's in there. I couldn't take the phone ringing any longer so I answered it. It was like a storm after that." She looked around the office. "I'm not supposed to be here, am I?"

"I don't know, but I can find out. May I?" The phone was ringing again and the woman answered it briskly and told the caller to wait. She dialed three numbers and spoke to someone on the other end just as efficiently. She sat back down.

"If you're a relative of Alistair Golden, he and I had an arrangement. I was to work for him until I could find something closer to home. He represented me in a court thing last week, and I don't have any money." She flushed and stood up when the woman smiled at her. "I'll just go now. If you see Mr. Golden, tell him I'll make other arrangements to pay—"

"Sit down, Miss Lawrence. My son is on his way here now. We'll get this straightened out."

Bronwyn didn't sit, but continued to the elevator. She was getting out of there before they had her arrested for something. The doors to the elevator opened just as the door to the office behind her did, and she slipped into the elevator. She looked up to see a gorgeous looking man staring at her while Mrs. Golden spoke to him. The doors shut just as he started toward her.

On the ride down she leaned forward, put her hands on her knees, and tried to deep breathe. Bronwyn was terrified out of her skull and was dizzy from it for the simple reason she did not want to go to jail. She was so fucked. Bronwyn took off the badge she'd been given that morning, planning to hand it to the guard at the security desk if she made it that far. A feeling in the pit of her stomach had her thinking she wasn't going to make it.

When the doors opened she knew someone had called them. She stepped out and tried to judge the distance from where she was to the doors and freedom.

"I can just go. No harm, no foul." Stan Flores, the security officer from earlier, shook his head and asked her to step back into the elevator. "Seriously. I would really like it if you just moved out of my way and let me go. I don't want…I don't want to hurt you, but I will if I have to."

"Miss Lawrence, you're not leaving here until someone from the top floor says you can. If you give me any trouble I'll handcuff you and take you up at gun point." Gone was the nice man from that morning, and in his place was a man on a mission. "Step back into the elevator and we'll both go up and see what's going on."

She hesitated just long enough for him to put his hand on his gun. Bronwyn wasn't afraid of guns, but she didn't want to be arrested again either. She looked at the door and took a step toward it when he pulled out his weapon. She felt her hackles rise as she raised her hands in the air. "Please don't do this. Let me just go and I'll never come back." He pointed to the elevator and she went in it. He never put his gun away and she never lowered her hands. What a great fucking way to lose a job she'd never even been trained for.

CHAPTER 2

Alistair was at the elevator when it opened. He was smiling, but dropped the smile when he saw her. She was pissed off and looking at the gun pointed at her as if she was expecting to be shot at any moment.

"What the fuck are you doing? Put that away." He pulled her out of the elevator and pushed the button for the doors to close. "Come on, Bronwyn. I'll take you to my office and apologize a thousand times for this screw up."

"I can just go home and I'll find another way to pay you. I swear I'll pay you every cent." She still had her hands up, so he pushed them down and sat her in the first chair he came to. It just happened to be the one in front of Ryland's office.

"You didn't do anything wrong. And I know you'll pay me back." Her eyes rolled to the back of her head, and he caught her just as she was going to fall forward. Alistair shouted for some help, and his mom and Ryland came running. "She's fainted. That fucking moron Flores had a gun on her. What the hell kind of place are we running here when women we hire are accosted like that?"

A wet washcloth was handed to him and he slapped it none too gently on the back of her neck. She tried to lift her head and he pushed her back down and glared at his brother.

15

He had to take his anger out on someone, and Ryland was the perfect target for it. "You had to scare her off on the first day, didn't you? You just couldn't stand the fact that you didn't know that Colette wouldn't work for you and that I'd found you suitable help in the meantime." His brother started to speak, but Bronwyn lifted her head again and he shoved her back down. "You should be horse whipped."

The shrill whistle made him leap from Bronwyn. He'd heard men whistle like that, but never a woman. He smiled at her when she stood. Damn, but this girl had spirit.

"You will not shove me around like an old, unwanted piece of furniture."

Ryland told her to sit down and shut up, and she stepped close enough to him to touch.

"And I am not a dog to be ordered about like one either." She stomped to the elevator again, and before she could touch the button, their mom stepped behind her.

"You've been treated poorly by my family. I'd like for us to start over. Could you please come and have a seat? I'll make sure that the two idiots are well away from us before we talk."

Alistair started to speak, but Bronwyn spoke to him first. "I will pay you back, but I won't be brought up on false charges again. All I did was answer the phone."

"I know, and if you'll come to my office we'll get this straightened out." He glanced at Ryland. "He's my brother. You were answering his phone, and from what Mom says, doing a great job of it."

"You said I was to be in some sort of work pool. That guy downstairs brought me here." Alistair nodded. "Is this where I was supposed to be?"

"Yes. I'd like for you to work here for the week. I know that—"

"Do I get any kind of say in this?"

Alistair looked at Ryland and wanted to brain him.

"I should have some say over who works for me. I do own this company."

"She'll work for you or I won't." Alistair turned to his brother. "You say one word, one single word, and I will quit now. There are nineteen of your projects sitting on my desk right now. If you want them taken care of, I would suggest that you go to your office right now and shut the fuck up. I'm tired of trying to deal with your temper."

Ryland turned, went into his office, and slammed the door. When Alistair turned around the doors to the elevator were closing and Bronwyn was gone. He snatched up the phone and barked for someone to stop her when she got off the elevator. "And the first person who pulls a gun on her will be unemployed before they put it back in their holster." He looked at his mom when he hung up. "There are days when I wish I had gone into business for myself."

"No, you don't. Go down and take the girl to lunch. She said she'd been here since around eight-thirty. It's past one now. She's probably starving. I'll meet you both at the deli across the street in five minutes."

He nodded, went to the other elevator, and pressed the button to go down and try to clean up this mess. Alistair rubbed his head. Ryland needed help, and he needed to have something go right for a change.

When the door opened, she was standing there waiting. When she tried to hand him her badge he took her arm and led her from the building.

The deli was busy, but he had a table reserved for lunch and just asked to have two people added. They were shown to his table a few minutes later. Bronwyn sat, but she refused to order, so he ordered for her.

"This is my treat if that's what——"

"You think I give a damn if it's your treat or not?" She looked around when he did and lowered her voice. "You said it would be fine. You said I'd work for you and no one would give me any problems. Having a gun pointed at me was a big fucking problem for me."

He nodded and felt his mouth twitch. He had no idea why he thought it was funny, but he was having a hard time not laughing. Besides, he was reasonably sure she'd knock him on his ass if he did laugh. Fortunately, his mom showed up before he could speak.

"You won't have any more problems with Ryland. I had a word with him and——"

"If you think I'm going back to that bedlam then you're nuttier than I am. In the event it escaped your notice, I quit. And I won't be going back there for any amount of money."

Alistair liked this girl, and knew that if she didn't work for him she'd have to go back to working where she'd gotten into trouble in the first place. And shot. He shook his head and took her hand when she started to stand.

"You signed a contract with me. You either work for me where I say or you go back to where I first found you, or to jail." She paled and glanced at his mom. "No one knows anything that you and I have talked about, and I'll keep it that way provided you do as you said you would."

"That's blackmail, and makes you no different that the man who got me here in the first place."

That hurt, more than he could imagine it would have, but he shook his head. "It's business. You signed the contract and I get what I want." Alistair didn't look at his mom, knowing she'd be mad at him. "What's it going to be?"

She didn't answer as their food was delivered. She looked at the food in front of her and didn't say a word. Then she nodded. He could tell that she wanted to say more, much more, but she picked up her bag again and stood. "I'll work and you'll get your money even if I have to sell myself on the side to get it to you." She looked at his mom. "You did a bang up job on raising this one. You must be proud."

As she stormed out of the restaurant, he nearly stood up to go after her to make her apologize to his mom. His mom stood up too and told him to sit down. He started to glare at her when he thought better of it. "She had no right to speak to you that way." He'd decided he was going to hunt her down and tell her all deals were off when his mom spoke.

"I've never been so embarrassed in all my life." He reached for her hand but she slapped him away. "You and your brother should be beaten and then beaten again for good measure. The nerve of the two of you fighting over her like a bone. You should be ashamed of yourselves."

"Us? She insulted you. I won't have her—"

"You insulted me, you jackass." She motioned for the waitress and asked her to box up hers and Bronwyn's lunches. When she had done so, his mom stood up.

"Mom, I never meant to insult you. She started it by telling you that you should be proud of the way you raised us. You did a great job and she had no right to say that to you."

She sat down, but never put her purse down. "You think about the way she was treated by my sons, you and your brother. No one came to train her, she answered a phone for nearly three hours without help or training, she had a gun pointed at her, was brought back up to the offices after trying to leave with her dignity, and you stripped that from her the moment you ordered her to come here with you. And your brother?" She stood up. "I'm ashamed of both of you."

Alistair sat there with his own lunch in front of him for over thirty minutes. His mother was right...they had treated

Bronwyn badly. Paying for the lunches, he took his own with him as he made his way back to the offices. He stepped off the elevator in time to see Bronwyn answer another call. Liz was sitting next to her.

~~~

Bronwyn saw him get off the elevator and turned away. She was going to work for him, but she didn't have to like him. And right now, she hated him. Putting the phone into the cradle, she looked at Liz when she stood up.

"I'm sorry, Mr. Golden, there was a miscommunication. I thought she was coming to my office and the officer brought her here. When she didn't show I thought she was a no call no show and—"

"And she's sitting right here." Bronwyn flushed when they both looked at her, but before she could say anything else the phone rang. She picked it up, this time with the correct greeting. She heard the two of them talking softly but not what they were saying, so she ignored them. When she hung up Liz was gone and Mr. Golden was sitting across from her.

"I'm sorry for the way you were treated. If I was half the man I thought I was I would have met you in the lobby and brought you here myself. I dropped the ball."

She looked at the notes she'd taken from Liz.

"You're supposed to say you forgive me."

There was humor in his voice, but she wasn't in the mood for it. "He pointed a gun at me. You said I'd be safe here. You told me…no, you promised me that no one would treat me like that again."

"Yes, I did. And I'm sorry about the gun. Are you all right now?" She nodded. "Bronwyn, look at me. Are you all right? Did you go to the doctor again?"

"I'm here, and I work for you from nine until five. I don't have to report to you about my health or my wellbeing." She looked at him. "You said yourself in the courtroom, we're not friends. I owe you money and that's all this is."

He sat there for two more phone calls. One he showed her how to redirect, the second one he told her to tell the caller that the company had a standard policy on that issue, and he would need to make an appointment through the company lawyer.

"Bronwyn, what you did for me that night…I wish you would just let me help you without all of this. I told you before that I owe you my life."

She stiffened, and then tried to relax when it hurt.

"Bronwyn, please—"

"I have a job to do. If you don't mind, I'd like to do it. And as for the other, I didn't do anything. I was just in the wrong place at the wrong time." The phone rang again and she snatched up the handset like it was a lifeline.

As he walked away, she reached into her bag and pulled out the pain reliever that Sindy had shoved at her before she'd left. She wouldn't be able to sit there much longer if the pain didn't recede soon. Taking a handful of them, she swallowed them down with a bottle of water she'd brought with her. The sandwich from earlier was still sitting untouched on the desk.

By four o'clock she was near tears, she hurt so badly. Thinking about cutting out of seeing Mr. Golden, she walked to the bathroom down the hall to see if her wound was seeping again. Blood stained her shirt and, even though it was dark blue, she knew that someone could see it if they looked. Pulling on her hoodie again, she made her way back to the desk to find the other Mr. Golden standing there. He looked anything but pleased to see her.

"Are you injured?"

She didn't move from the doorway. When he came toward her she backed into the wall behind her and moaned at the shooting pain. She held onto the wall behind her while he looked at her.

"You are hurt and bleeding. What is the matter with you?"

She shook her head, not able to speak through the pain.

"I asked you a question and I want an answer."

"I'm just fine and dandy," she snapped, and glanced at the clock over her desk. "It's almost five o'clock and I'm supposed to meet with the other Mr. Golden. No one showed me how to put the phones to the service, so either you show me or you do it, but I'm out of here."

He stared at her for several seconds before he went to the phones and pressed buttons. She didn't know what he was doing and didn't ask. This man was a prick, and she decided she didn't like him overly much.

When she started toward Mr. Golden's office, he followed her. Trying her best not to show she was hurting, she walked as close to the wall as she could without touching it. When she told the secretary that she had an appointment with her boss, she was asked to wait. She stood while her boss watched her.

"You should call me by my first name. It'll make it easier on you when you have to tell which one we are."

She didn't care what his name was, nor did she ever think that there would be an occasion where she'd have to speak to them together.

"Did you hear me?"

"Yes. I just don't care what your name is. You're both Mr. Golden to me." The secretary told her she could go in now. She started toward the door, and he followed her. "I'm seeing him, not you. I put in my eight today with you."

"I want to speak to you both." He opened the door for her and she watched as Alistair Golden came toward her from his desk. "Go inside, please."

As Alistair approached her, she wondered what the hell they wanted, but she wanted to go home and crawl into bed and never wake up. When Alistair asked her to sit, she looked at the chair with longing, knowing that she'd never get up if she sat.

"She's bleeding."

Bronwyn looked at the other Golden, Ryland, and before she could deny his claim he continued.

"She's in a great deal of pain too. Though she won't admit it, she's afraid to sit down because she more than likely won't be able to get up again. What happened to her?"

"None of your business." She looked at Alistair. "What did you want to see me about? I'd like to go home."

"Ryland, she's all right, or so she's told me several times. I'm handling this. She needs some rest is all."

She glared at them both, and she had a feeling that something more was going on, especially when Alistair looked at her sharply.

"What happened to you?"

She looked at Alistair, who nodded at her, then back at Ryland when he asked again.

"Something is hurting you and you are bleeding. Badly, I would say. If I don't get some answers I'm going to call the police after I call an ambulance."

She sat down. Weak with worry that he'd do just that, she dropped her bag to the floor and looked at Alistair. He sat too and handed his brother a file. "It happened three nights ago. She was bartending at the bar on Tenth when a man came tumbling out and fell on me. Another man came out quickly after him and fired three shots. Bronwyn took two that were

Kathi S. Barton

meant for the first man and saved my life by killing the man with a bat that had been under the bar."

"You bastard." She tried to stand up, but couldn't. "You said that no one would know. You told me that I'd never have to let anyone know what happened after the judge had it tossed out."

"Let me see." She looked at Ryland when he stood up. "I want to see the wounds. Where are they?"

"Go to hell. I'm not showing you shit, and where do you get off thinking that I would?" She looked at Alistair. "I'm finished. I'll get you the money I owe you somehow and then I'll be—"

"Be quiet."

She snapped her mouth closed and glared at Ryland when he turned to Alistair.

"She's my mate. I didn't...Christ, when I smelled the blood I came out of my office to see what she'd done. Then she came down the hall and I could smell it was her. I got close enough to smell all of her, and she's my mate."

"Christ." Ryland nodded at Alistair and both men stared at her.

She had to get out of there, and right fucking now. Standing up cost her, but she was moving to the door when hands wrapped around her waist and over the wound in her side. Screaming out in pain, she turned and hit him. She was falling now and knew that when she hit, she was going to hurt worse than ever. Closing her eyes against the impact, she slipped away when she was grabbed again. This time she felt the wounds tear open.

24

CHAPTER 3

Ryland watched her sleep. She was so still that he was worried for her. Twice now he'd gotten up to make sure she was still breathing, even though he could hear her heart beating in her chest. He touched her hand and was amazed at how cold she still was. He moved back to the chair when the door opened. His mother and two of his brothers stood there, in addition to Alistair.

"She all right?"

Ryland nodded at his mom.

"Why don't you go home for a while and we'll stay with her? Doctor Myers said she'd be out for a few more hours."

He and Alistair had talked while they waited on the ambulance to come. He wasn't to tell anyone what she was to him. Alistair had agreed, but only after he made Ryland promise that he wouldn't wait too long. Their mom was going to be pissed enough as it was. He wasn't too happy either.

"I'll stay with her. She works for me and I rode in with her." That sounded lame even to him, and he decided to change the subject. "She have any relatives that we should notify?"

"The nurse pulled her file when we got here. There's a next of kin to notify. I didn't hear what the woman was to her, but her name is Sindy Wilson. The nurse seemed be familiar with Miss Lawrence."

Ryland nodded at his brother Brock.

"You think she's been in here a lot?"

Ryland didn't know, but when he'd pulled up her shirt to look at her wounds he'd had to take several deep breaths. She'd lost a great deal of blood, and there were enough scars on her ribs to tell him that someone had used a whip on her recently. He looked over at her again and wondered who she was.

"I'm going to tell you how I came to meet her. She will be pissed, but I think under the circumstances, we should all know." The door opened and his last two brothers walked in. Alistair smiled. "Good. We're all here. I was going home from work three nights ago when I walked past the Red Rose. I could hear the fight going on inside and was just about to cross to the other side of the street when a man came tumbling out and fell on top of me."

"Did you get your suit dirty?"

Ryland glared at his brother Jules and he apologized.

"I never seen a man so particular about his suits as he is, was all I was saying."

"Well, don't say anything else unless you can be constructive. This is serious. She saved his life." He looked down at her again then looked at his mother. She was staring at him oddly.

"The man had been drunk, but not hurt. Bronwyn came out after him, yelling at him to get home and that she'd called a cab. Seconds later, another man came out just as she was helping me to stand. He was holding a gun and telling the first man that he was going to kill him. Bronwyn tried to reason with him, but he pointed the gun at the first man just as he fell. She stepped in front of me and took both shots." Alistair sat down. "Had he hit me in the position I was in, he'd have shot me in the head. Both shots. She didn't drop, and at first I thought he'd missed us both. She had a bat in her hand and she hit him. He dropped then and hit his head. The police said he was dead before he hit the ground. But she stood there after he fell and turned to look at me. Her face was covered in blood and she was pale. As I took a step toward her, thinking she was in shock, she put out her hands and told me not to touch her. She said for me to leave so that no one would know I was there. She said I was too pretty to be in that part of town and to run."

"You stayed with her?"

Alistair nodded at Ryland.

"What did the police say when they got there? It was self defense, correct?"

"They arrested her even as she was being put in the ambulance. The medic came to find me before they left. She was awake and pissed." Alistair smiled. "She has a very colorful vocabulary when she's upset. She was pissed at me."

"Whatever for?"

Ryland looked at his mom, who looked at each of them before continuing.

"Why was she mad at him? All he'd done was stay with her until help arrived."

"Because I told him to get the hell away from there." Everyone turned to Bronwyn when she spoke. "You said no one would know. You lied to me like everyone does."

Ryland started forward, but she waved them all away. She tried to sit up, so he pushed her back to the bed. When she pulled on the cord to summon a nurse, he turned on the light above her head. Christ, she looked like shit.

When the nurse came in, she told everyone to step out. He sat down and looked between the nurse and Bronwyn. He wasn't going anywhere until he spoke to her. When she realized he was staying, she looked at the nurse.

"I have no insurance and I'd like for you to bring me a set of walking papers, please. The Against Medical Advice ones. I think they're on your desktop."

He was a little disconcerted that she knew where they were, but before he could tell the nurse that she wasn't going to need them, the nurse left.

"What do you want?"

"You're not leaving here until you're released by a certified physician." She laughed and he bristled. "I'm serious. If I have to tie you to that bed then that's what I'll do."

She tossed the covers off and sat up. He could see sweat as it beaded on her upper lip, but he didn't move to help her. Maybe if she hurt badly enough she'd lay back down. The nurse came in with a handful of papers and a pen. He took them from her and told her he'd take care of them. Bronwyn didn't say anything, but nodded at the nurse when she looked at her. Ryland had a feeling that a great deal was said with that nod. He just didn't know what.

"What do you want?" Her voice was low, but he heard her. "I don't have anything of value, and I certainly don't want anything to do with you. I want to know what you want."

"I'm.... You saved Alistair. I owe you." She nodded and he thought she understood. "You're going to have to stay here until you're well, then we'll talk about compensation for you helping him."

"No." He waited for her to explain just what she thought she was telling him no for, but she said nothing more and slipped off the bed. He didn't want to be impressed by her, but it was hard. When she started walking toward the bathroom, he stood up.

The door behind him opened and a small woman came in, and as she walked past him he smelled her. He sat down when she told him to. Christ, she was another tiger.

~~~

Sindy wrapped her arm around Bronwyn and helped her to the bathroom. She didn't have to tell her she was hurting, it was on every line of her body. When Bronwyn grabbed onto the sink, she nodded at her and Sindy stepped back and closed the door. She took several deep breaths before she turned to face the man. When she turned, she bowed before him and stood up.

"You're her friend."

Sindy nodded.

"Then she's aware of us. Of what we are. How long have you known her?"

"Ten years. She and I sort of grew up together. And yes, she knows what I am, and more than likely what you are as well." She looked at the door to the hallway. "Is that your streak out there?" A streak was what his family was called when they were all together. Sometimes they were also referred to as an ambush. He and his family apparently liked streak much better as he didn't correct her.

"Yes. I'm the dominate male and I lead." He stood up, but she didn't back away like he'd thought she would. She could see it in his face.

"She won't come to you. I don't mean to say she won't come to you easy, but not at all if she's what I think she is to you." He sat down and looked to the door. "She knows what will happen if she becomes your mate. She saw it with mine."

"And your mate, where is he? Shouldn't you have come here with him?" She laughed and told him no. "Then you should have him come to me. I would like to have a word with him about living here without my knowledge."

"He's dead, thankfully. And I know the rules as well. I don't have to subject to you either because of my status as a widow." Sindy turned when the door opened and she went to her friend. She was weak, but moving. They were headed toward the door when the man stood in front of them.

"You don't want to piss her off." Sindy looked at Bronwyn then back at the male in front of her as she continued. "She may look weak and helpless, but she is far from it. And whatever she doesn't do to you, I will."

He laughed, which was what most men did when Bronwyn defended her. Sindy asked him again to back the fuck up. When he didn't move Bronwyn pushed Sindy away from her. Sindy knew what was going to happen, and was glad that he was in a hospital. He might need it.

"You were asked to stand down. Now I'm telling you to do so. I don't want to hurt you, but I will, fucktard."

"You know what I am, what we are. You should know that you're my mate and that I take that role very seriously. I would like it very much if you would let me take care of you while you're hurt. We can talk later about how you will affect my life."

Sindy laughed. She couldn't help it, and laughed harder when he turned to her.

"You, I will deal with at a later time. This is between her and me."

Sindy bowed again. He was a leader and she had no choice in the matter…it was in her DNA. But she knew her friend and what she was capable of. She'd seen her hurt others before, kill too. She tried again to reason with the male.

"She'll hurt you if you don't stand down. I wish you would get your head out of your ass and step back before she does what comes natural to her." He gave a condescending grin that made her want to sock him. "It's your funeral then."

The room tightened. She was sure that the male felt it because he looked around, then at her. Sindy shrugged. She took another step back when the energy level reached higher; the room seemed smaller. When Bronwyn reached out and touched him he simply looked at her, for all of a second. Then he went flying across the room and hit the door behind him, hard enough to crack it in the middle. Bronwyn's hand swept across the air and he was airborne again, this time landing in a heap by the bed. Sindy grabbed her before she collapsed.

"He's going to be pissed when he wakes up." Sindy nodded and opened the door to see the rest of his streak coming toward them. "Shit. I won't be able to walk if I have to deal with them too."

"I've got this one." Sindy pulled out a gun and pointed it at them. "It's loaded with silver and a cyanide chaser. You come near me and I won't hit you in a vital place, but one that will shatter the capsule in the center. Even in this nice hospital, they won't be able to save your asses."

Bronwyn leaned on Sindy heavily, and she knew that she was nearing the last of her energy. Sindy kept the gun pointed at them as she backed them to the elevator. Bronwyn could smell the hot scent of blood, and knew that she had reopened her wounds. As the doors closed, Sindy let her slide to the floor while she tried to think.

"They aren't coming for us. They're taking care of the ass in the room." She could tell Sindy was still scared. "Cyanide chaser? Where the hell did you think that one up?"

Sindy laughed. "I saw it on one of those shows I watch. I'm sure it's not possible, but it worked. That big one, the blond that looked at you like he was afraid for you, is that the guy you saved?"

"Yeah." Bronwyn tried to climb back up the wall to stand. "I'm not going to make it out of here. Put me in a room and I'll take care of the rest."

Sindy nodded. When the door opened she looked for a lone nurse and asked her to come see what she'd found on the floor. As soon as the nurse was close to Bronwyn, she touched her.

"I'm in need of medical help. No one must know where I am. You'll give me the care that I need, being careful not to get caught. Your patients must come first after you get me into a safe bed and stitched up." She let go of her arm and looked at Sindy. "If I die, you know what to do."

Sindy nodded and helped the nurse pick up her friend. She was in a room ten minutes later when the streak came down the hall. Sindy simply closed the door and locked it. No one would get to Bronwyn, not if she had to kill the lot of them to keep her safe.

Sindy watched Bronwyn breathing. She knew that she'd normally need at least eight hours of rest after doing what she'd done to the male. But with her loss of blood and injuries, she knew it would be a great deal longer. Sindy owed Bronwyn her life and wouldn't cause her any harm or allow her to be harmed.

Sindy's husband had been an abusive bastard. She'd been mated to him because he'd wanted her, and her own streak had been invaded. She never loved him, and realized years later that he'd never been anything but an abusive prick. Not that he hadn't abused her from the beginning of their time together, but since her dad had been nearly the same kind of male she assumed they all were. But her husband didn't need a reason. He had beat her nearly every day for some minor thing, and Bronwyn never knew until one night when he'd attacked Sindy in front of her.

Sindy begging her not to hurt him had Bronwyn backing off to let Sindy handle things. But when he grabbed Bronwyn and threw her against the wall, all bets were off. She'd come back at him with a hammer at first, hitting him twice the number of times he'd hit her. Finally, he'd hit her in the throat. Bronwyn had gone down, but came back up with her power and killed him. Her anger getting the better of her, she'd thrown him against the stone fireplace several times before Sindy had to slap her to bring her back. Sindy's mate was nothing but shattered bones and blood. She had told Bronwyn to leave, and then she called the male of her group.

"You didn't do this, Sindy. You're neither smart enough nor strong enough. Who killed him? You have to tell me." The male had been put into place when the streak had been taken over. But there was a dead man in Sindy's house and she had nothing to tell him.

"I told you, Dana hit me so many times that I passed out. When I came around, he was like that." She turned to look at his body and shivered. "What kind of monster could do that?"

He'd ignored her during the funeral and had the members of the streak help clean up the mess. A week later, he told her to leave. She had expected it sooner, and had already packed her things.

"The streak is talking, and they don't know what you called up to do this to him. Everyone here knew he hurt you, but he was your mate and it was his right."

She nodded and glanced at Bronwyn, who had come to help her pack.

"It's the law that you belonged to him and there was nothing I could do about it, nothing I would have done about it. If you won't go to another male, then they want you gone as soon as possible."

She was gone by nightfall and had never looked back. She'd moved into an apartment and asked Bronwyn to live with her. Bronwyn stayed with her sometimes, but never moved in. Sindy knew that Bronwyn was protecting her from whoever was chasing her.

"I'll be all right." She got up to go to Bronwyn when she spoke. "Go home and rest. I'm going to feel bad if you stay here when all I'm going to do is sleep this off."

"You might need something. There is only one nurse to care for you and not one on each shift. I can just rest in the other bed." She was already shaking her head. "Bronwyn, if they find you here, they aren't going to take it nicely that you hurt their male. It's against the laws of our kind to harm your mate."

"He's not my mate, and I'm not a tiger. I'm a sort of regular person. Now go home, and in the morning you can come help me out of here." She moved on the bed slowly. "Sindy, thank you for coming."

Sindy brushed at the tears and nodded. "You would have and have done the same for me. I can't let my secret weapon get away from me."

Bronwyn closed her eyes and smiled before speaking. "He's not dead, but he is pissed off. His brother…Brock is telling him that he should just leave it alone. I don't think he will."

Sindy doubted he would either. The man was just like her husband had been…king of shit, and everyone beneath him was just that, beneath him. The hair on her arms rose when she felt another cat near. She watched the door, and when no one tried the handle, she looked at Bronwyn. She was asleep again. Gathering up her things, she left the hospital and went back to her apartment. There were three messages on her phone, but she ignored them in favor of some sleep. Climbing into the bed, she wondered if Bronwyn would be able to get away from her mate, or if she would be trapped like Sindy had been.

CHAPTER 4

"She's not here. And if she is, she's not anywhere we can find her."

Ryland looked at his brother Alistair and thought he was happy they couldn't find her.

"And since you *fell* on something wet on the floor and broke five ribs and your leg is bruised up, you can't help us look either."

He didn't know what had happened. Well, he knew, but his mind wasn't believing it. She had tossed him around like he was nothing but a flea. He looked at the room, similar to the one she'd been in, and knew that no one had been in there with them other than the cat, and he knew that, whatever it had been, it hadn't come from her. Christ, Bronwyn had a power that frightened him a little.

"Are you listening to me?" Ryland shook his head at Alistair. "I asked you if she said anything before you *fell*? When they came out of that room Bronwyn looked like she'd been about to fall over; and that other cat...who the fuck was she?"

"A widow. She said that she knew the rules and that she didn't have to come to me for permission to live in this area. Is that right?" Alistair nodded and smiled. "You know this is not the least bit funny. She's my mate, damn it. She needs to be brought to heel."

Alistair shook his head. "What century were you born in again? Women are not brought to heel; they are loved and nurtured. Maybe if you got our ass out of your office once in a while you'd know that."

"I know what I expect from her, and if she doesn't like it...." Ryland took a deep breath and let it out slowly. "I don't have a clue what women want or need. Especially one like her."

Alistair sat down and stared. "What do you mean 'especially one like her'? And you can stop with the falling shit. If I tell you my story, you'll tell me yours. Deal?"

Ryland nodded, almost afraid to hear the real story of what had happened that day. "She isn't human, is she? She's something more."

"More would be a good starting point. Bronwyn.... Christ." Alistair looked at the window before continuing. "Bronwyn didn't use a bat. There wasn't one there and she told me there was and I wanted to believe her, so I said there was one. She lifted him up without touching him. And when he smashed—yes, that's what she did, smashed him against the wall—I heard the bones break. Bronwyn looked at me afterwards and I could feel her touching my mind, but there had been no connection between us. Not like we have as tigers; it was just a touch. Then she told me to go away."

"She couldn't make you see it her way, so she had you leave the scene." Ryland wanted to find her and asked her if that was true, but needed to get out of there first. He tried to stand and told Alistair to get him signed out.

"You're going to find her?" Ryland nodded. "Then you might want this. It's her jacket. She left it in my office when she left yesterday. I think it has her scent, as well as the other woman's. It might not bring us to her, but the other one will know where she is, you can count on it."

Yeah, and Ryland had a bone to pick with her too. She had warned him to back off, but had never said why. She had to know that he'd be hurt…well, she had told him that it was his funeral, but he hadn't realized she wasn't kidding. He wondered now why he was still living when he looked at Alistair.

"She couldn't kill me."

Alistair laughed.

"No, I mean, she wanted to. And I think that other woman knew she was going to as well. But she didn't. Why? Is it because on some level she knew that she couldn't?"

"Or you were just lucky. I've seen her in action too, remember? I think if she wanted you dead, there would be no stopping her. She's amazing. And I bet she can do more with it. So much more than maybe she knows."

Ryland thought Alistair might be right. He limped to the bathroom to strip down and shift. He would have done it at home, but he had a feeling that he needed to find Bronwyn now. When he closed the door behind him he heard his brother talking to someone. Shifting, he felt his cat take him and he moaned at the feeling.

It had been a long time since he'd shifted because he wanted to and not because of the waning moon. And when he did it then, it was to satisfy the cat in him and not much more than that. He put his paws up on the counter to look at himself in the mirror.

His fur was golden and his black stripes stood out boldly on his coat. His white chest was full and thick, and he twitched his tail to look at it. He wanted to snarl at himself, but knew that he'd bring down a whole shit ton of trouble and end up in the zoo if he did. Hopping back down, he shifted again, glad now that his kind had no time restraints on how long he had to remain a cat before he could shift again. Looking at his ribs, he saw that he was still bruised, but no longer sore. His leg was better as well. One of the many wonderful things about being a were.

He came out to find his brother talking to his mother and Brock. He looked at them when they frowned at him. "What is it? Did you find her?"

"Not Bronwyn, but we do know where she lives." Brock looked at his mom then back at Ryland. "You're not going to like it."

Ryland didn't think he would like a great deal of what she did, but was going to try and keep an open mind. *Where she lives*, he thought, *is going to be the least of my problems*. He began pulling on his shoes as he asked his brother to explain.

"She lives in one of the buildings on Western." He stopped in the middle of tying his shoes and looked at Brock. "Yeah. Those buildings. At least that's the address she put on her paperwork at the courthouse when Alistair represented her. She supposedly lives in one of the ones that's been condemned. I looked it up; there are nine other people using the same address."

"We own those, don't we?"

Ryland nodded at his mother's question.

"Well, that should make it easier for you to find her. I still would like to know what you plan to do with her once you do. The girl was back at work and when she left, she was hurt. What happened in that space of time?"

Alistair cleared his throat and looked at him. Ryland rubbed his hands over his face in frustration. This was not going to go well. "She's my mate. And she ended up here because I grabbed her when she tried to leave. I hadn't meant to hurt her, but she was bleeding and I could smell it. When she went to Alistair's office I lost my…it didn't go well and she was leaving. I didn't want her to."

"So you bullied her. And she tried to leave you and you decided that you were bigger and meaner, so you simply used your brute strength to get what you wanted."

Ryland didn't even try to argue. What she said was true. "Yes, ma'am. And when she was here, the same thing happened. She wanted to leave and I tried to stop her. But she…she left, and now I need to find her." His mother sat in the chair across from him. "Mom, I'm so—"

"Don't you dare tell me you're sorry. I don't want to hear how sorry you are. You hurt the one woman in the world that is supposed to love you, and you tell me you're sorry." She stood up to pace. "I swear to you, I've never been so…. If you were younger I'd beat you with a belt. That poor girl has saved your brother's life, and you treat her…. I'm going home. I don't want to speak to either of you until you both fix this."

Alistair looked at her when he realized she was talking about him too. "I didn't do anything to her. He's the one that—"

He shut up when their mom simply raised her finger to him. Both of them had fucked up. Ryland more so than his brother, but he had as well. They looked at each other when their mom left the room. Brock went with her to drive her home.

~~~

Bronwyn woke with a start. She heard a voice and moved quickly to get away from it. Then Sindy came into focus. She laid her head back down on the pillow and assessed the damage to her body.

"You've been here for two days. I was beginning to worry. How are you feeling?"

She nodded at her friend.

"Good. We might want to go when you get dressed. I think that male is looking harder for you, and I think he has his streak looking too."

Bronwyn stood up, but wobbled. If she'd been here for three days counting the first day, she hadn't eaten in all that time either. Going slowly, she asked Sindy if she had a candy bar or something she could eat until she got home.

"I brought you some clothes that you'd left at my house and a sandwich. I also brought you a cooler full of juice. You need to have the liquid." Bronwyn took the offered bottle and drained it, and then the second. "I guess you needed that."

"Yes." Taking the clothes, she went into the bathroom, searching the hospital mentally for the nurse. Bronwyn told her that her services were no longer needed and thanked her. As she dressed slowly and with care she thought she might feel better, but she was still hurting. By the time she came out, she was exhausted and drank two more bottles of juice.

"I borrowed a car from someone at work. I hoped you'd be up and about today, and, if not, I was going to try and wake you." Before Bronwyn could tell her not to do that, Sindy continued. "I know it's dangerous to wake you, but it's getting harder and harder to come and go in here. There are cats everywhere."

She pulled on her shoes and laid back. "Do you think you can take me home? I will be okay if I can get there."

"I don't know, Bronwyn. You're still pretty weak. Are you sure you don't want to stay with me a few days? Just in case?"

She wanted to more than anything, but even though Sindy was a widow she still had to abide by the laws of the streak. Bronwyn knew that the male wouldn't stop until he found her or until she killed him. Either way, she was not becoming a "thing," as her friend had been to her mate. And no man would hit her and live to tell about it. She didn't give a shit how good-looking he was.

"I'll be fine. I just need a little more rest and then to figure out how to pay that lawyer back. I might need you to run interference with him when I make a payment."

Sindy nodded.

After eating the sandwich and the chips, Bronwyn polished off two more juices. It was really good if she had pure juice and not the fake kind, but she was simply grateful that Sindy had thought to bring her any. They left the room as Bronwyn kept searching for any cats.

Sindy was right...there were a lot of them around. Each time one would look their way, she'd distract them. It was easy at first, but by the time they got to the car Bronwyn was lucky she could give Sindy directions to where she was staying.

Once there, she got out and searched again, but she was beyond exhausted and couldn't do much more than look to see if any were in her part of the building. Going inside, she sat down on her only chair and told Sindy to go on home. When Sindy reached her car and started driving, Bronwyn erased her memory of where she'd been and why. Sindy knew she did it and knew it was because, if asked, she wouldn't be able to tell them anything. Bronwyn went to her bed, lay down, and passed out again.

The next time she woke up it was daylight. Bronwyn moved better, but not well enough to leave the building. She was just getting out of the shower and dressing when she felt the cats nearby. Standing still and holding her position, she closed off anything that would lead them to her. The door wouldn't be there and there would be no scent of her. Bronwyn waited a good thirty minutes until they left before she moved again. Moving to the kitchen, she nearly screamed when she found the male sitting at her table.

Bronwyn didn't even bother asking him how he'd found her. She didn't care, but as soon as he left she was going to leave as well. Starting a mental list of things she would take and those she would leave, she reached into the cooler on the counter and pulled out the last juice that Sindy had brought her. He spoke from behind her.

"This place is slated for the ball next month. Where will you go then?"

She didn't answer.

"I'm assuming there's a reason why you're hiding out and not getting a real job like most people."

"I have a job. It's real and pays what I need. I don't buy up people's homes and businesses to make money, but I get by." She leaned against the counter and ate the last half of the sandwich she had. It wasn't enough to replenish what she'd used, but it would do her for now. She moved toward the other room, pulled out one of the many first aid kits she'd put together over the years, and opened it.

"Do you need help?"

She didn't answer him, but pulled up her shirt to look at the dressing that Sindy had put on her before they'd left the hospital.

"Christ, how are you even walking around?"

"I use my feet just like most people do." Bronwyn took out clean padding and put it against her skin. As she was wrapping gauze around herself he told her to stand up, that he'd help her. Bronwyn didn't move, but continued to care for herself. She'd have to go out soon and hoped that she'd be able to get somewhere and back before she was too tired to care.

"I'd like to talk to you, but somewhere where there is electricity and running water."

She looked around her place and noted that while there was a little dust, it was clean and she had running water. It was freezing cold, but she had it. "I'd like for you to leave, but it looks like neither of us is going to get what we want." She put tape on the end of the gauze and pulled her shirt down. "Say whatever you came here to say and get out. I don't want you around me."

"I got that at the hospital." He sat on her chair and she on the large crate she used as a sort of all-purpose table. "I wanted to tell you to...ask you...to come back to my place with me. You need care and you won't get it here."

"You just saw for yourself that I am getting care. So that shoots that argument all to hell. Next?" She watched him fight for control of his temper. "What do you think you're going to be able to do? Bring me to your home and rape me? No, thanks. I won't be a whore for any male, human or otherwise."

"I wouldn't rape you." He sounded so indignant that she nearly smiled. "And you wouldn't be my whore, as you called it, but my mate. If I wanted a whore I'd find one. But you're my mate."

"Whatever you want to call it, it's all the same to me." She stood up and began putting things in a pile she was taking. It wouldn't be much, but there were things she wanted near her. She turned to him when she heard him stand.

"You have a power that I've never seen before. I wanted to talk to you about that as well. I want to know what else you can do besides toss around a grown man like he's nothing to you."

"I don't know what you're talking about. And just so you know, you don't mean anything to me." She picked up her bag and winced when she moved funny. "I've seen your kind before. You want, you take. You need, you take. You want to fuck it, you rape it."

"Who?"

She looked at him.

"Who did this to you? Or was it Sindy? Is that what happened to her mate? You helped her become a widow?"

She didn't answer, but continued gathering her things. When she went into the kitchen again, she pulled down the box of tampons and dumped it on the counter. Opening each packet, she took out the money there and dumped the rest.

"Impressive way to hide money. How much do you have?"

She handed it to him, all but thirty dollars. He started to hand it back after counting it.

"Give it to your brother. Tell him I'll get him the rest when I have it."

He said he wasn't going to take her money.

"Good, because it doesn't belong to you. I said your brother."

Bronwyn walked to the door, opened it, and waited for him to precede her; when he didn't, she left first. She was halfway down the stairs when she heard him cussing and coming after her. Bronwyn wasn't going to run; she would really hurt herself if she tried. But when she got outside the building, four black SUV's pulled up and she had to make a choice.

Stop where you are, she told the male. *If you come out, they'll kill you and leave your body here as a reminder to anyone that sees us to not say anything. And for Christ's sake, don't shift.*

Who is out there?

She didn't answer him as the first man got out of the front car. She dropped her bag and lifted her hands. He stopped moving toward her.

"Now Bronwyn, you know that if you run I'm going to hunt you down again. You really should have stayed at the lab and let me finish what I started. You're going to have to work extra hard to pay for all the damage you did."

"Fuck off." She glanced to her right when the man from another vehicle moved toward her. She moved her hand and he fell against the black vehicle with his head denting the metal.

She felt them before she saw them, and she tried to warn them away. But she was too busy trying to keep herself from getting killed when the streak of tigers entered into danger. When the one behind her snarled, she closed her eyes. They were so fucked.

CHAPTER 5

Ryland saw what she'd done to the man at the SUV and had nearly cheered her on, but he watched as three more men, all of them armed, came in from behind her. She'd be captured or dead, whichever they were there for, in seconds. Ryland reached for his brothers and told them to come to him. Their response was immediate and without question.

"What the fuck is that?" The man who had been threatening Ryland's mate started for his car when his door slammed shut in front of him. He worked frantically at the handle while screaming at the other men to save him. Ryland made a run for him just as his brothers went after the other men.

He knew she was keeping them from being shot. He also knew it was draining her. When he was grazed by a bullet, just singeing his fur, he turned to see if she'd let it happen on purpose, but she was saving his brother Jules from being shot. The man holding the gun had been lifted nearly ten feet when she dropped him. Then she looked at the man Ryland was chasing.

He'll leave a bad taste in your mouth if you kill him. I'm reasonably sure he's got poison for blood.

Ryland tripped and nearly stopped to turn to her when she made the joke. He nearly had the man when he finally got into another vehicle. Ryland leapt up on the hood and could smell the bite of urine.

He wet himself.

She laughed, and he did turn to her then. He'd never heard her laugh before. Christ, it was like wind chimes. When she looked at him, Ryland saw her waver. She was getting too weak to protect them much longer. Calling his brothers, he had them step up their game and run off the men who were still alive. The dead were on their own. He moved toward her.

She staggered again, but managed to save Brock this time. He would have been shot in the head had she not knocked the shooter into the building and killed him. She was playing for keeps. Ryland had a feeling these men were as well.

The last car pulled away and he stood near her. He still hadn't shifted back, and he wouldn't until he was sure she was safe. He nodded to his brothers and thanked them.

Jules walked up to her and bowed. *She saved me. I saw the gun aimed at me and was sure I was dead.* He looked at Bronwyn before bowing to Ryland. *Christ, she's fucking beautiful.*

When she collapsed, he moved to catch her. He was too late to do that, but he did manage to keep her from falling too hard. She landed on his big body, and he waited to see if she would try and roll off him. When she didn't, he slid from under her gently and moved to shift back into his body and clothes. Alistair and Neal stayed with her, guarding her until he returned.

When everyone had shifted and dressed, he asked someone to bring him his car, and asked Keith to go into the building and find her a blanket or something to wrap her in.

He knew she was going to be weak. What he didn't know was how to help her.

"Do you know where that woman is? The one that was in the hospital with her?" Alistair replied that he did. "Can you contact her? Tell her that...I'm not sure what to tell her, but tell her that Bronwyn was attacked and she fainted again. Ask her if she'll come to my house and show me how to care for her."

Alistair stood staring at him for several minutes before he spoke. "Who are you, and what have you done with my brother? Ryland would never have said the words, 'can you,' and 'ask her.' He would have said get her and tell her. So again, I ask, who are you?"

Ryland wasn't amused and told him so. "I was scared shitless just now, and maybe I hit my head. I can demand if you want. Those men were going to take her to a lab."

Alistair didn't say anything as he looked around, then spoke when he looked back at her in Ryland's arms. "They'll come back. Maybe not today, but they'll come back here. She knew it too. I heard her telling us to back the fuck off, but you were telling us to protect her. That's the only reason we didn't stop when she commanded. She's your female no matter what she thinks."

Ryland had heard her telling them to leave. She'd even told them that he'd said so, and he was pretty sure that had he not been talking to them as well, they would have. The car pulled up, he carried her to it, and put her in the back. When Alistair got in the front to drive, Ryland stayed in the back with her.

"She's not going to be happy to be with you again."

Ryland agreed.

"Can I make a suggestion?"

"Yes. But I'm pretty sure I know what it is. You think I should try not to be a bastard."

Alistair looked at him in the rear view mirror and nodded.

"I thought of that too. But she's going to be spitting mad, and I'm pretty sure I'm going to lose my temper again."

"Then I hope to Christ your will is all in order. She doesn't strike me as the ask questions first and kill you later sort of person."

Ryland silently agreed with his brother. He looked down at her. Jules was right…she was beautiful. Her hair was a light curly red. She kept it up in a ponytail, he noticed, and wondered how long it was. Would she spread it out over his pillow when he made love to her? Frowning, he tried to think of anything but her and bed in the same thought.

Her skin looked soft, and he touched it just below her eye. There was a bruise there and he wondered when she'd gotten it…today, or when she'd saved Alistair? He looked at her hands and wondered what made her so powerful. She obviously had a great deal of control, or she would have killed more than she'd hurt. And she had hurt them. He looked at Alistair when they got on the highway.

"Do we have anything on those men? Plate numbers or anything we can search?"

Alistair said he'd had Brock pull VIN numbers off all the vehicles that had been left behind, as well as plate numbers. "I'm going to have someone from the offices run them when I get back tomorrow. I want to find them as badly as you do."

Ryland started to agree and thought of something. "Don't do it from the offices. They might be looking for someone to do that. We'll run them, but not from any of our computers." Alistair nodded. "Do you still know that computer guy, the one that helped us a few years ago by putting up the firewalls?"

"Yes. I'll give him a call and have him see." They pulled off the highway and onto a street he was as familiar with as his own hotel room. "I didn't think taking her to your hotel was a good idea. You have maids and other people in and out of there all the time, and someone might say something. Here is better."

It might be safer for her, but not for him. His mom knew who she was to him, and would more than likely go to great lengths to throw them together. When they pulled up in front of the house, a gurney was brought out and he looked at Alistair.

"I wanted her to prepare a room for her...and one for you. She also called in Uncle Joey so that he could come over and look at her. He said he'd be honored to see to your mate."

"She's not my mate." Alistair laughed and nodded. "She's not. And she might never be either. She's stubborn and pigheaded."

"Yes," Alistair said as he helped bring her things in. "You and she are a perfect match. Though I don't think I'd say that to her. She would probably hurt you."

Ryland was afraid of that too.

~~~

She woke and knew that she was no longer at her home. Nor was she in the hospital. Opening her eyes, she looked at the man in the chair who appeared to be sleeping. The second she moved in the bed, he stood up.

"I have to pee." She didn't have the energy to be polite...and with him, she didn't feel she wanted to be, not really. When he came to the side of the bed, she glared up at him.

"I want to help you. I'm going to pick you up and carry—"

"No. Christ, don't do that. When you pick me up, it...you bend me. And that puts pressure on my sores. Just back off and let me do this myself. I've been doing it for a long time." She tried to sit up.

"The bed is softer than you're used to." She glared at him again. "I can help you. Stop being so damned stubborn and let me."

Bronwyn knew that she had no choice. It was either he helped her or someone else did, and she had a feeling he wouldn't go and get anyone else for her, so she would wet the bed. Not really an option, but she was contemplating it seriously.

"You wet the bed and I'll make you tell my mom you ruined her mattress." Ryland laughed. "And no, I can't read your mind, though you seem to be able to communicate with me and my streak."

She was getting desperate. "I'm going to sit up, and you just stand there and keep me from falling over when I do. And if you try anything, they'll be picking parts of you up for decades."

She couldn't do it. When he leaned over her she stiffened, not sure what he was going to do to her. When he put his arms under her shoulders and at her legs, she lifted her hand to shove him away.

"Just move your legs to the side of the bed as I pull you up. I can do it slow or fast. Tell me which you prefer." He was so close she could see the dark lashes at his eyes and the colors of his eyes. "Bronwyn?"

"Fast." Before she could take a breath, he had her sitting there, her legs over the side and her feet touching the floor. Taking several deep breaths, she knew that if he did anything to her now, she would not be able to stop him.

"I'm going to put my hands on your hips. Can you put your good arm on me?" She nodded. "I'm going to lift you straight up."

She looked at him. Sweat beaded on his forehead and he looked to be in a great deal of pain. She wondered why he was hurting and asked him if he'd been shot.

"No. Touching you like this…it's not easy." She looked down, hurt. "Bronwyn, it's not that I don't want to touch you. Christ, you have no idea how much I want to…but I know that you hurt."

So, she thought, *if I wasn't bleeding and weak, he'd take me.* Bronwyn nodded to him and put her hand on his shoulder. She felt his hands slide up her thighs and cup her ass. Bronwyn wanted to tell him to back the fuck off, but she was suddenly standing.

The sudden move made her scream. There was no help for it. Every part of her body hurt, and she dug her fingers deep into his shoulder. Her breathing hard was making her dizzy, but when he took a step back, she took one forward. Not soon enough, they were at a door.

"I'm going to sit you down on the commode. Can you do…can you fix your under things?" She reached down to tear them from her when she realized she had none on. She told him that.

His entire body seemed to expand. She felt his hands tighten on her ass and she knew he was going to rape her, damn how hurt she was. When he sat her down and backed away she swayed, but caught herself before he could touch her. Looking up at him she could see that he was hard, his cock thick against his jeans.

"I'll be right out here." He walked out and closed the door behind him. She stared at the door for a full minute, trying to think what she'd done wrong, then realized that she needed to take care of business.

Standing was easier in the bathroom. She was close enough to the hard counter that she could brace her body against it as she shuffled to it. Washing her hands and face took a lot of energy she didn't have, but she felt better. He told her through the door that the new toothbrush was hers, and there was paste on the counter.

Brushing her teeth felt wonderful, but took the last of her strength. Moving to the door, she reached for the handle at the same time it opened, and she looked up at him. Not saying a word, he pressed his body to her and lifted her to him, cupping her ass again.

"Let me go." She tried to struggle, but he held her tighter. She looked up at him when he stopped suddenly.

"I'm getting you to bed. I'm not joining you in it. Once I get you there I'm going to cover you up and leave you." He looked over her shoulder. "I don't know who hurt you like this, but it wasn't me."

"Not yet anyway."

His jaw clenched. He took her to the bed and reversed the process he'd used to get her up. As soon as she was stretched out, he tossed the covers over her and went to the door. He stopped before going out. "I'm a prick most of the time. And I can be a real bastard. But I don't rape innocents. Nor do I have to force myself on women." He turned to her. "I want you, I won't deny that, but I'm not going to take you without you asking me to."

"Never." He nodded and left the room. The door closed softly behind him. She waited for several seconds for him to come back and demand his rights as her mate, but he didn't.

Bronwyn tried to relax so that she could rest. Her body hurt. She'd used a great deal more energy than she had to spare to keep the streak of tigers from getting killed…and to keep herself from being taken. Cunningham was getting quicker at finding her.

She knew it was because of Sindy…had known for several months that he was watching her every move. Sindy had no idea, of course, because Bronwyn knew that if she even suspected it, she'd have Bronwyn erase all memories of her and tell her never to contact her again.

Bronwyn thought of the male. He was going to get her…she knew it as much as he did. Males took what they wanted and no one could stop them. She knew this firsthand from living with Sindy's parents when they'd been her foster parents.

Mr. Daniels had been a male at one time as well…not the sort that determined his sex, but the head of his household. He was still demanding and brutal. The only reason that Bronwyn had stayed was so that she could protect Mrs. Daniels. She was the only kind person Bronwyn had ever met. But she was also a lesser female to her husband.

He would expect her to have his dinner on the table at five o'clock regardless of her health. Bronwyn had often told her to let him fend for himself; he didn't work, but sat in the living room all day, and even made her bring him his meals if he didn't feel like getting up.

But she wouldn't make him get his own meals…nor would she leave him. When Bronwyn had suggested it, as she had to Sindy several times over the years, they would both simply tell her it wasn't done. Males were there to protect them and they, as lesser females, were there to serve. But Mr. Daniels had not done anything when the larger group of tigers had come through. He'd given up his wife and daughter to the first male that had said he wanted them. That was how Sindy had, at seventeen, been with her abusive male. And Sindy was the only one to have survived the takeover.

Now Bronwyn was in the same situation. A male had come, and had decided that she belonged to him. She wouldn't go easily, and if she had to mate with him she'd kill him after so that she had the same status as Sindy. A widowed female had no rights, but no one would want her anymore.

Closing her eyes, she thought of Cunningham and the lab he'd taken her to years ago. He'd tricked her into going with him and then, when her parents had been killed, had taken custody of her. It had taken her nearly four years to get free of them and him. Four years that she'd never forget.

CHAPTER 6

Ryland went to the kitchen. He was on fire for her. Need didn't just coil in his belly, but his entire body. When his brother Keith walked in the door, Ryland knocked him back out the door and into the yard with his fist. Thankfully, Keith fought back.

When Keith came up off the ground he hit Ryland in the face. Blood poured from his mouth as he dropped his shoulder and rammed his brother in the gut. After that it was a free-for-all, each of them knocking the other down and then getting up to serve the same treatment back to his sibling.

Ryland felt the first spray of water hit him in the back and turned in time to have it hit him full in the face. Keith took advantage of this distraction and took him down from behind. Within seconds they were both being hosed down, and the water was fucking cold. Ryland started to tackle the person with the hose, but then realized who it was.

"Are you finished beating the snot out of each other?"

Keith started for their mother, still in the heat of the moment, but Ryland caught him by the shirt collar. He looked ready to do battle when Ryland nodded to their mom.

"He hit me first." Ryland looked at Keith when he spoke. "What the fuck? I walked in the door and you nearly took my head off. I didn't do shit to you."

"Keith, go in the house and get cleaned up."

He looked like he was going to argue with her, but finally nodded and walked by Ryland, nearly knocking him over with his shoulder as he moved past him.

Ryland watched his mother. "He's right. I did start it." She nodded. "I needed to…I needed an outlet, and he was the first person I saw."

"So I suppose it was a good thing I wasn't in the kitchen when you came down."

He flushed.

"How is she?"

"Asleep again. I had to help her to the bathroom. She's hurting pretty badly." He looked at the woods behind his mom's house. "She thinks I'm going to rape her. She's expecting me to."

"I don't doubt that she is." He looked back at her. "Do you know the streak that the other girl is from?"

"No. I tried to look up her name, but it's either been taken from the roster or she was never marked as a part of it." He went to the deck and sat down with her when she asked him to. "What do you know about it?"

"Long ago, there was a law. Actually, I think it might still be on the books. Anyway, it was a law that said, basically, that any male could take what he wanted. Females were considered lesser. They were referred to as that, lesser females. And if a larger streak, or ambush as they were referred to in the books, came to a small establishment, they could and would expect to be given whatever they wanted. It's referred to as a razing."

He looked at her as she finished. "You don't mean that even if the females were already attached they had to go to the male, do you?" She nodded. "That's barbaric. That means...." A thought occurred to him.

"Yes. I can see by the look on your face you realized that even if there was a young female, she too would be given to the males. I'm sure it happens today even, but we never, your father and I, never practiced those older laws." She looked at him. "That young woman from the hospital, is her name Sindy Wilson?"

"Yes. I tried to find her in the books, but as I said, she wasn't there."

She took something from her sweater pocket and handed it to him. He read the headline and looked at her.

"Her mate was murdered. His body had been crushed, the article says, by an unknown force. It says that this young girl was beaten as well and was not a suspect in the murder, but she was asked to leave the streak. They were afraid she was able to bring up a demon and they didn't want her there any longer." She pointed to the name of the paper. "We used to get these publications that the Tiger Corporation put out for years until this one came out. Your father called them up and told them that he wanted to be taken off the list. We never got another one."

"Bronwyn killed him."

She shrugged.

"She must have been saving her friend. So she knew what he'd been doing to her. She also must think that all of us are like him."

"All men, I would say. Think about the man who tried to take her this morning. You saw the scars on her back. You and I both know she's stubborn and he probably had her beaten, thinking he would break her." She rocked in the swing a few times. "I wonder why she hasn't killed him."

Long after his mom went into the house, Ryland stayed seated where he was. He looked up when Keith approached him, and stood when he offered his hand. Ryland apologized to him, and Keith nodded.

"Mom said that she wants me to help you." Keith laughed. "She said you might need help charming your mate. She said that you're a little rusty at being around the fairer sex."

He looked at the door, then back at his brother. "I might be, but taking advice from my baby brother isn't going to happen. I thought I'd go to a better source than someone who can barely keep it in his pants even in a public place."

"That only happened one time." Keith grinned. "Okay, three times, but I didn't want to leave anyone disappointed. The ladies love me."

Ryland snorted. "I just bet they do." He joked around with Keith until lunch, and then decided to find the other woman. He'd been hesitant in looking for her, afraid that she was being watched by the men in the cars. He went into the house to call Alistair when he heard a crash from upstairs. Running full tilt, he took the stairs three at a time and kicked the door open.

"What the fuck is the matter with you? Can't you just come into a room like a normal person?" Bronwyn was sitting on the edge of the bed with a trashcan in her lap. Before he could answer or figure out what was going on, she leaned her head into the can and gagged. Christ, she was sick.

When she lifted her head and glared at him, he moved toward her. His mom came in behind him, and Ryland looked at her and asked her for some crackers and tea for Bronwyn.

He looked at Bronwyn when she told his mother not to bother.

"What did you give me? Before, when I was asleep? Did you have a doctor give me something?" She leaned into the can again and he could hear her retching. This time, when she lifted her head, his mom handed her a wet cloth. "What was it?"

"Oxycodone. He said it would help with the pain and healing." He took the can from her when she lay back down. "Are you allergic?"

"I can't have drugs. Not of any kind, and especially not any narcotics. If I do then…well, you can see what happens. Christ, I fucking hurt." He looked at his mom when she came out of the bathroom loaded down with linens.

"You'll have to stand up, love. You've sickened in the bed. Your shirt will need to be changed as well." His mom removed the blankets as she spoke. "Help her up, Ryland. She needs to be cleaned up."

"Mom, I don't think—" She raised a brow at him again and he nodded and looked at Bronwyn. "Come on. I'll take you to the bathroom and help you."

She was weak again and he could see it. Lifting her up as gently as he could, he knew there was no way she could have stood up like before. Besides, he wasn't sure he could do it again. When she moaned he knew he was hurting her, but there was little to nothing he could do now.

He sat her on the counter and held her as he reached into the shower to turn on the water for her. She was covered in vomit…it was even in her hair. When she moaned as he tried to take her shirt off, he tore it off her. His breath caught at what he'd revealed.

She wasn't beautiful. He could see now that the word did not do her justice. She was magnificent. Her breasts were large and full, and her waist tiny and tight. He moaned when her nipples hardened. He wanted to cup her into his hands and taste her. Then he saw the bandage and hated himself for his thoughts. She was fucking hurt, and he was an animal wanting to rut her.

Leaning her back against the mirror, he took off his shirt and emptied his pockets. Toeing off his shoes, he reached down and took off his socks. He tried to will his cock to behave, but it wasn't happening. Picking her up, he stepped into the shower.

She clung to him as soon as the water touched her. He adjusted it to a warmer setting and set her onto her feet. She was wobbly and he was afraid of dropping her, so he held her as best he could. Holding her with one hand, he reached up, opened the shampoo with his teeth, and poured it over her head. Setting it back, he washed out her hair. Then he did it again, just because she didn't fight him and he loved the feeling of its silky mass running over his hands.

When he'd rinsed her hair clean, he reached for the sponge and poured soap onto it. Washing her proved to be hard because she was fighting him. Every time he tried to wash her more private areas, she would wake and hit at him. Finally, he pressed her against the wall and lifted her chin to look at her.

"I need to help you get cleaned up. You can help me this way, or I can step out and fill the tub, and do it that way. Either way, you're going to be washed by me." She nodded and he finished cleaning her up. She even lifted her foot up when he asked her to. Christ, even her toes were sexy.

When he stepped out he grabbed a fluffy towel and wrapped it around her hair. Then he started on her body. By the time he got to her feet again, he was sweating. He'd never touched a woman this much in his life without it being sexual.

Lifting her again, he took her to the bedroom, where his mom was just finishing making the bed.

"Juice." Ryland looked down at Bronwyn. "I need juice. It'll help me heal so that I can get out of here. He'll return for me."

His mom said she'd get her some and left. Ryland didn't put her in the bed, but went to sit in a chair with her in his arms. Foolish, he knew, but he was loath to let her go. He began talking when she struggled.

"The man that was at the building? Who was he?" She didn't answer, but then he hadn't expected her to. "He tried to kill my family. I need to know who he is."

"I need to leave as soon as I'm able, or he'll be more than happy to make your acquaintance. He's a man who gets what he wants." He looked down at her and he noticed that her eyes were closed. "I'll need to have my bandage changed. Do you know where my bag is?"

"I don't. I know someone picked it up, but I haven't seen it since we got here." He stood and put her in the chair. "I have some shirts here. I'll put one on you."

"I have my own clothes." He grinned at her tone. "Can you just find my bag so I can fix me?"

He opened the second drawer and took out a shirt, one of his favorites. His mom had given it to him years ago. He brought it to her and held it out. She looked away.

"I'm pretty sure that in your current state of weakness, I could make you put this on. But I would rather not have to fight you for it. But if you refuse even that, I could go get the first aid kit from my bathroom and change your bandage while you're naked. That too has its merits." She jerked the shirt from him. "Thank you."

Turning his back to give her privacy, he glanced at the mirror over his dresser. He wasn't going to watch her get naked, he told himself, but he wanted to make sure she didn't fall. He knew he was lying to himself even as she pulled the shirt over her head then slipped the towel from under it. He turned around when his mom came back.

~~~

Sandra watched her son with Bronwyn. He was gentle and teasing. Even when the girl snapped at him he laughed and joked with her. She couldn't believe the difference in him. When he pulled the wet bandage off her wounds Sandra was afraid he was going to snap.

"I was going to call your friend Sindy, but thought she might be watched." Bronwyn winced and didn't say anything as Ryland continued. "She could stay here with you if you want, but I would have to have her stay here. I don't know if she works or not, but if she were followed then that man would know where you are. What did you say his name was again?"

"I didn't, and you damned well know I didn't. And Sindy does work. She and I worked together at the hospital until a few years ago when I was...." Sandra looked at her and knew that whatever had happened for her to no longer work there, it had been because of the man that had come for her. "And you're right, she is being watched. He has her followed. It was my fault that he found me like he did."

"You knew he might, yet you used her to take you there because I had pissed you off." Ryland nodded. "Like I said before, I can be a prick."

Sandra burst out laughing. Ryland had said that as if he'd been telling her that he was going to the market. He winked at her. She stood up when he did, planning to help him put the bandage back on Bronwyn. She watched as he held the dressing in his hand and stared at the girl.

"It would be easier to wrap around you if I stood you up and held you. Mom can wrap you and that way, it would be secure."

Sandra took the gauze and dressing and held it while Bronwyn was lifted up by Ryland. The wounds were cleaner and they were looking good. Sandra had been a nurse before the boys had started coming, and hadn't forgotten how to look for infections or anything else from gunshot wounds. Ryland spoke softly to Bronwyn as he held her.

"I grew up in this house. I loved it here, but when I graduated from college I felt as if I should move out. Mistake. I knew that from the very beginning."

Sandra stumbled at his admission.

"My mom says I need a house. I live in a hotel. I own it, so it's not really all that much of a hardship, but I've just come to realize that I've been missing out on some things."

"I have never lived in my own house. I lived in foster homes, always in a bunch of other people's houses, until I turned fifteen and another streak came and took them away." She looked at Ryland when she said that. Christ, the girl had been there when the razing had taken place. It wouldn't have been any easier on her than it had been the lesser females.

"How many did they kill before it was settled?" Sandra had asked before she thought about the memories it might make. "I'm sorry, it must have been hard for you."

"They took Sindy first. She was the same age as me at fifteen. Five males got to 'try her out,' they called it, before she was placed with Dana. Mrs. Daniels was next. There were other women in the compound, but I wasn't able to get away to help them. Not that I could. The male said it was his right to have what he wanted. He took it all, including Sindy's father. Mr. Daniels simply dropped to his knees and let him tear his throat out in front of us. He had said it was his honor to have the male take his wife and daughter before all the others."

"Christ." Bronwyn looked at Ryland then, staring into his face as she finished her tale. Sandra wished that she'd left him to it, and had run away and hidden from the story instead of listening to it.

"I was human, so they only beat me. The whip. It was the first time I'd had it used on me. Not the last, mind you, but it was most definitely the first. One hundred lashes. I don't remember much past the first forty or so, but I knew that he'd given them to me. Then he chained all the other women there…only those who were too old to breed, ones that had some ailment or another. Each of them died, all of them suffering as they did. Then the children were murdered. Ten little boys who might grow up to be like their fathers, he said, lazy tigers that hadn't defended their streak. He sat them in a nice row and then walked behind them and broke their necks. And do you know what he did then?" Ryland shook his head and Sandra held her breath. "He killed Mrs. Daniels because she had whimpered when the children were dragged away."

Sandra stepped back when Ryland pulled Bronwyn into his arms. The girl was suffering more than she'd ever known a human to suffer. When Bronwyn pulled away and staggered to the bed, they let her. Lying down, she covered up and closed her eyes.

"I'm really tired now. If you won't mind leaving the juice, I'll drink it in a bit." She rolled to her back as she continued. "He's going to come for me…the male and the man from the lab. They are working together to find me so that I can help him fund another worthy project with the money he'll make in selling me to the highest bidder."

CHAPTER 7

Sindy could smell the male before she saw him. He was close enough that her hair danced on her arms. When he stepped out of the room and in front of her she nearly took off running, but he spoke first, very softly so that no human would have been able to hear.

"I came to tell you that I have Bronwyn." Her entire body went weak with relief. She grabbed the wall as he moved toward her, but she stopped him and pointed to the room he'd come from. He nodded and stepped back in as she made her way down the hall with her cart of meds.

As much as she wanted to stop and go to him she knew that she was being watched. He must have known as well because he never came out to get her, but waited. She went into the room to hand the other man in the bed his medications. Sindy spoke to him in the same way he had to her in the hall.

"Is she all right? Does she need anything?" She handed the man his water. "She needs plenty of juice after an ordeal. She will drink any kind, but pure juice, just squeezed, helps her the most."

"I'll take care of it. You heard about the incident at the abandoned buildings, I take it." She told him she had. "I was there. She used the last of her strength to save us from ourselves. They were going to take her again."

The curtain where the male stood fluttered. Sindy asked the man in the bed if he needed anything and he asked for water, please. She said she'd be right back and left. It really was the job of the aides, but she needed to ask more about her friend. When she returned, he stood in the opened curtain and handed her something.

"It's a cell phone. My brother Keith is somewhat of a nerd, and he fixed it so it will bounce all over and no one will be able to track it. The number to the house is programmed in it, as are my other brothers' and mine. Their names are there as well." She handed him a small package also. He looked at her when he opened it.

"She's hurt, right?" He nodded. "It's all she can use as a pain medication. It works a little, but not if she's hurt.… Is she hurt badly?"

"Yes. But she's getting better. She sleeps a lot and, as far as I can tell, only gets up when she needs to use the bathroom."

Sindy nodded.

"She will be pissed because I came here."

"You know she will. But I'm glad that you did. I was worried the moment I saw those trucks on the news. I knew that they'd come for her." She wiped at a tear. "I thought they had her."

"They won't get her. I swear to you, they won't." Sindy only nodded, but he took a step toward her and she backed up. "I won't hurt either of you. You have my word. I know…she told us what happened the night you were razed. She said that.…"

"If she told you that then she would have told you that I won't trust anyone. I doubt very much she will either. There are days when I…when I wished Dana would have killed me too."

He nodded, but didn't try to tell her that she was wrong to think that. Nor did he say that things would be better. Bronwyn did the same thing every time she said something like that to her.

"What's his name?"

She looked at him, confused.

"She said that the man who is trying to take her is in with the male who killed your family."

Sindy felt faint. As she staggered back he helped her to the chair. He kept saying he was sorry, that he'd thought she knew. She finally looked at him, tears running down her face. The man hadn't hurt her, but that didn't mean she would trust him completely.

"I don't know the name of the man in the lab. She might have said, but I don't remember." He nodded, and she knew that he was aware she was lying. "The male, the one that did those things to her, his name is Crawford, Forest Crawford. He has a large streak. He calls them an ambush. If he finds out you've been with her, taken her, he'll kill you."

The male stood up and looked down at her. He was frighteningly huge, but for some reason Sindy wasn't terrified of him. Afraid yes, but not terrified. She stood up and watched him. He turned to her and nodded.

"I'm Ryland Golden. Do you know where the Towers are?" She nodded. "You come there if you're hurt or need something. Someone there will find me. No matter what it is, I'll get it for you." She told him to keep her friend safe. "You can count on that. She's as safe as she'll ever be now."

She moved down the hall and gave out medications for two more rooms before she saw him slip out of the room. He never acknowledged her in any way, not even to look in her direction. When he stepped onto the elevator she moved into another room and handed the woman there her little white cup and water as she wondered about him. She had a feeling that if anyone could save Bronwyn, this man could more than likely come out on top.

Sindy stopped by the grocery on her way home. She'd changed into her street clothes so that she wouldn't be stopped by every mother with a sick child. Being a nurse was what she'd dreamed of all her life, but there were times when she wished she had chosen another career.

She saw the man just as she put the lettuce in her cart. He'd been in the parking lot yesterday, too, when she'd left. Looking at the cucumbers, she pretended to try and decide on which one when he moved to another lane. Maybe she was just being paranoid. When she went to the counter to pay she didn't see him anymore and went out to load her things into her car. That's when she saw him in the next lane over.

Sindy got everything loaded into her car and took the cart back up. Looking into her purse she saw the phone that Ryland had given her that morning. Sindy reached in and then looked back at the store, trying to act like she'd forgotten something. Going back inside, she walked to the other end of the store to stand in front of the meat counter.

Smiling at the butcher, she asked for two pounds of ham. She hated ham, but there was a mirror over him, and she watched as the man she thought was following her moved to the end of the aisle, then back again when he saw her. Afraid now, she pulled out the phone and pressed the first name she saw.

"Hello Mrs. P. It's me, Sindy. You asked me to pick up some ham and a bottle of wine, but I've forgotten the brand."

"This is Alistair Golden. Is this Sindy Wilson?"

She laughed and said yes, it was a lovely day.

"Good girl. Do you need for me to come and get you?"

"Oh yes, that would be great. I was just about to go home and fix me some leftovers. How about we go to the pizza place next door to Market's? I'll treat."

"I'm on my way there now. I'll meet you inside. Don't come out once you get in there. I know the owner and I'll give him a call."

She nodded, but realized he couldn't see her and told him she would.

"Hang up now, but don't run out of the store. Take your time. That way I can get inside before you do."

Sindy lingered over the wine, not really seeing anything but the colors. Picking one at random, she moved to the front with her luncheon meat and her wine. As she started toward her car, she thought better of it and took the bag to the pizza place next door. She moved inside and was being seated when a large, burly man came toward her. Sindy nearly screamed when he touched her arm.

"Alistair is out back. See that table over there?"

She nodded and glanced at the woman who was sitting at the table that he indicated.

"Go and sit there. The man who's following you, what's he look like?"

She described him as best she could and then sat down. As the woman across from her reached for her hand, Sindy heard the door open.

"No, don't look. Just look at me or the menu. You can hand me those packages if you'd like." Sindy handed her the bag and smiled. "I've not had an all the way pizza in months. This was such a lovely idea. We'll have to do this more often."

Sindy nodded, and when the waitress came to them the woman ordered for them both. She smiled at her when their waters were brought to them. She started to tell the woman she had to meet a man named Alistair when Ryland and two more men sat down at another table.

"He's not in here yet. He was on the phone when I came in." She nodded at Ryland when he spoke. "Sindy, this is my mom, Sandra Golden. When you pretended Alistair was a woman, we had to improvise. She wanted to help."

"He might hurt her." Sindy looked at Mrs. Golden. "He will hurt you if he knows what is going on."

Two more men joined Ryland and the others. She realized that they were all related and that she knew them…the streak from the hospital. These were his brothers. She started to stand when the door opened again, and she sat down.

The tension was tight. When their pizza came, while Sindy only picked at her piece, Mrs. Golden ate three slices. She grinned at her when she started to speak.

"Would you be a dear, Sindy, and help an old woman to the bathroom? I'm not feeble, but I do…well, I don't want my skirt to be caught in my hose."

They walked past the table where the man was sitting, and he didn't look up. They were in the bathroom when Mrs. Golden pulled out her cell phone and handed it to her.

"Is that the man from the store?"

She looked at Mrs. Golden, who nodded encouragement to her as she spoke to Ryland on the phone.

"I need to be sure before we do anything."

"It's him. Do you know him?" Ryland told her no. "He might be carrying a gun. I don't want to get anyone hurt if he's the real thing."

"You stay in there with Mom and we'll make sure whether he's the real thing or not."

She handed the phone back to Ryland's mother. "Mrs. Golden, what if he only wants my phone number or something stupid like that? What if he's nothing more than a man who wants to go out?" Sindy leaned against the counter. "He might not be anything."

"Its Sandra, honey, and if he's wanting a pretty girl's number there are any number of ways of getting it other than scaring the snot out of her. You let my boys handle it. They'll get him straightened out if that's all he wants."

There was a knock at the door and she stiffened. When the big man opened it and told them it was safe, she and Sandra went out. There was no sign of the man. She looked at Ryland.

"He was supposed to bring you to the lab so that you'd call Bronwyn and have her come and get you." She looked around, then back at Ryland when he continued. "He's not going to be coming back. And I'm afraid you'll have to come with us as well. They'll not give up."

She sat down again. This was suddenly too much. They were going to use her as bait to lure Bronwyn to them had it not been for this man. She looked up at him. "I'm afraid." He nodded and dropped to his knees in front of her. "They would have hurt her again, wouldn't they?"

"Yes. If they would have gotten you they would have. But they didn't. You were brave and smart. If you wouldn't have called, you'd be...." He didn't finish. He didn't have to. She knew. She would have been dead.

"His name is Cunningham. I'm not sure if I ever heard her call him anything but that. He works for a company called Better Future. They advertise that they make healthier foods for today's consumer. Whatever the hell that means."

Ryland nodded, looked at the men behind him, and repeated the information.

"There's something else you should know about Bronwyn. She is a lot stronger than you think. She can do anything to a person's mind, including manipulate it to her way of thinking."

~~~

Bronwyn saw Ryland there again when she woke. She sat up slowly and he smiled at her. She didn't trust that smile any more than she did him. He handed her a glass of juice.

"It's freshly squeezed. I wish I could tell you I did it, but my mom did. She said it was her pleasure to do so."

She sipped the orange juice and felt it race through her body.

"I want to speak to you about Sindy."

"She's none of your concern." She looked at him suspiciously. "What have you done? If you've hurt her or given her to one of your brothers, I'll kill you."

"We're going to have to work on your inability to say what you think. You should try to just come out and say it."

She flushed.

"She's here. As of two days ago."

"That's not possible. She would never come to your home, no matter what you did to her." She started to get up when he stood too. "I would like to speak to her alone. She's my friend and I want to make sure you didn't hurt her."

He sat on the edge of the bed and pushed her to the middle. When he lay down next to her, she tried to get to the other side, but he pulled her to him. The harder she tried to get away, the more she hurt herself. Finally, she just lifted her hands to toss him off her.

"Before you do that, you should hear what happened to her." She stilled. "I went to see her at the hospital. I wanted to tell her you were with me and that you were fine. Hurt, but mending. I also gave her a modified cell phone so she could call if she needed anything. A little over six hours later, she called Alistair."

"You led them to her." He shook his head. "Then how did they find her so soon after you went to talk to her?"

"They'd been following her for days. The man that had been tagging her at the store then at the pizza shop told us that he was supposed to snatch her from her home, but she'd gone to the store, then to the pizza shop first. He said that they had planned to use her to get you to come to them." Bronwyn laid her head down on his chest so that he couldn't see her tears. "He also told us that when they got you, they were going to have an auction to see who got to fuck Sindy first and then kill her. She doesn't know that part."

"You brought her here." He nodded. "Does she know where she is? I mean, did you knock her out and bring her here?" She felt him stiffen beneath her and started to pull away again to ready herself for whatever he had planned. But he rolled her to her back and laid over her. Her hands were lifted above her head and he held her there.

"I'm not a monster. I know you have no reason to believe me, but I'm not. I won't hurt you or her. I want you." He rocked into her and she felt his cock. "But I won't take what's not freely offered to me."

"You'll say that now, but men are all the same. They take everything." She was waiting for him to snap at her, anything, but he only stared down at her. She looked away and he turned her back to look at him.

"Who else besides Cunningham and Crawford did this to you?" His voice was low, and not the least bit hard like she'd come to expect. "This is more than what they did to you at the lab. This is more than what happened to you during the razing. Someone got you to trust them, then they betrayed you. That's it, isn't it?"

Bronwyn tried to turn away again. He was too close, his words too true. She looked at him then, tears falling from her eyes. All she wanted was for him to leave her alone…for everyone to just simply leave her alone.

"My mother sold me to them. When I was six. She used me up until then. I would go to her dealer with her and wait while she fucked him in front of me for the payment. Then he wanted more than her; he wanted someone fresh, someone that wasn't so strung out that they'd forget to eat for days on end and look like they'd not had a bath in weeks." She laughed bitterly. "She told him that instead of her giving me to him that I could do tricks. That's what she called them, tricks. She told him that I was talented in that I could make people believe anything I wanted them to believe."

"What did she have you do?"

She laughed again, pissed that even after all this time it still hurt her. "She had me make his dealers believe that they'd been paid. He would take me to the pick-ups and I would sit and color, all the while making them, the sellers, think that the scraps of paper they were getting in the cases were real money and that he was paying them. I tried to tell them that it wouldn't work. Someone was going to figure out that they'd been lied to and trace it back to them." She looked away from him again and he let her. "They came back a few weeks later. My mother and Santos were living it up with the cash they'd made from my ability. When the guy came to kill them…when he came to get what was his…."

"She gave you to them."

She nodded.

"How long were you with them before you killed them, Bronwyn?"

"Not even a day. I was taken to this huge house and…. They had killed them anyway. My mother and Santos, her dealer/lover. I knew it before I left. They told me that she'd be back for me once she had the money to buy me back...then I'd be free to go. In the meantime, I was going to do the same for them that I'd done for my mother. I'd had enough. I killed them all. I didn't mean to, but I didn't have any control; well, that's not true. I had some, but I didn't hold it back. I was found covered in blood the next day and put into a foster home."

CHAPTER 8

He held her until she fell asleep. Then Ryland got up and went to find his mom. He wasn't a momma's boy, but he knew there were times when he needed her. He found her in the kitchen making dinner.

She set a plate of cookies in front of him, and he picked one up and ate it while he tried to think how to start. She sat down across from him and handed him a glass of tea. He looked at her for several seconds before he reached over and took her hand into his. "How did I miss how wonderful you are?" She blushed and started to rise, but he asked her to sit. "I don't know how to be her mate without her wanting to leave me or kill me."

"You're not afraid of her, are you?" She laughed when he nodded. "Smart boy. She is a little intense, but I don't think she'll want to kill you so much after she gets to know you a little more."

"How long do you suppose that will take?" She seemed to be thinking on that pretty hard. "I don't know if I want to know now or not."

She got up and went to the sink. "Do you know that when your dad started making more money than we needed to spend in one week on bills, he offered to get me help? House help, he called it."

He didn't remember that, but he did just realize that his mom had never had help with the house and all of them. Ryland leaned back in his chair and looked at her. She really was a remarkable woman and he told her so.

"No. I was just…frugal, you could say. Plus, I was always afraid that the money would stop and I'd have to fire the poor person who had come to work for us. I knew that I couldn't put someone out of work because I was too lazy to do my own dishes."

"But the money never stopped. Why didn't you hire help later, after Dad passed away?" She shrugged. "Mom? Why not?"

"I knew that someday you'd find yourself a mate. I had hoped, I suppose, that she'd want to keep me around to help out; you know, sort of cook and stuff for her and you. Then as the years went by and you never seemed to want to find her, I decided that I'd simply care for you for the rest of my days." He started to tell her that he'd never want that when she continued. "I know that it sounds so silly, but my point is that I wasn't any better at being a mate than you think you might now be."

"How so? You raised us boys while Dad was away. You went to all the little league games, practices, and plays. Why did you think you weren't a good mate?" He looked at her when she turned toward him. "You think you failed Dad, not us."

"Yes. He was so…he loved to go to those fundraisers. I hated them. He loved being with the people who knew him. He was a good man, a wonderful father, but he was a good deal more sociable than me. I think he was disappointed in me."

Ryland stood up and led his mom to the office his dad had used. Ryland used it now that he was there more. He sat her at the desk and pointed to the pictures. "What do you see there?" There were perhaps a dozen or so pictures on the desk, all of them depicting varying stages of their lives. He noticed that there were a few recent ones, some that had been added after his father had died. That's when he realized that he had pictures on his desk at work, of his parents together with him, and of him and his brothers on a fishing trip. There was even one of them at the zoo as they stood in front of the tiger exhibit.

"Your father and you boys."

He looked at the pictures, picked up the same one he had on his desk, and was pretty sure it was on his brother's as well. He handed it to her. "This one. What do you see here?" She ran her fingers over the glass reverently and smiled. "He's looking at you as if he is the happiest man in the world. And he is looking at the woman he loves."

The picture was of the two of them. They were at one of the socials that she said she hated so much. They were looking at each other and laughing at what looked to be something just the two of them would understand. His dad had his arm around her and she had hers tucked into his shoulder. They looked so happy.

"He told me once that he loved seeing me all dressed up. He gave me those pearls that night, and told me that I would be the loveliest woman there. He said that it wasn't because of the necklace, but because he loved me." She looked up at him. "You treat Bronwyn half the way your father treated me and she'll be as happy as the two of us are in this picture."

She stood up and kissed his cheek. When she handed him the picture he sat down and looked again at the others there. He wanted to see his mate there with him, and children of his own. He looked at his laptop and moved the mouse. He'd been looking at houses and had stopped on this one. Ten bedrooms and five baths; it would hold his family and any children that he and Bronwyn had together. He took out his cell and called the realtor.

They talked for over an hour. He knew that Bronwyn was going to murder him, and more than likely his mom too, but by end of business tomorrow, if everything went the way he planned, he'd have his own home. He set the picture down on the desk again and smiled. Now he had to go and tell Bronwyn.

~~~

She heard the door open and waited for whoever it was to speak. It had taken her nearly ten minutes to get to the bathroom, and she wasn't leaving until she felt clean. She wondered how much water that would take. And there were some of her own clothes on the counter…clothes that Sindy had put in her bag when she'd left for work that morning to bring to her if she found her.

She shivered when she thought of what she'd learned from her friend. It was her fault. Bronwyn should have been there to protect her. But Ryland had saved her, his brothers and him. Even Sandra had helped and, according to Sindy, had had a good time too. When the knock sounded on the door, she stuck her head out of the shower.

"I'm almost finished. Who is it?" She heard him laugh and knew it was Ryland. "Go away. I'm feeling really good, and I don't want you to spoil it for me."

"If you hurry a little more, I want to take you outside and show you the new kittens that were born yesterday. And Mom is making her famous lasagna. She has garlic cheesy bread too." Her belly growled and she knew he'd heard it. "If you're really good, I'll give you my second helping."

She pulled her head back into the shower and washed up. She'd taken off the bandages before getting in, and she looked down at the wounds. They were healing nicely and, while she had numerous scars already, she didn't think these would be so bad. Someone had done a good job of stitching them up. She was bruised too, but those were fading now and she only looked slightly like a battered woman now, rather than one that had gone a few rounds and came out on the bottom.

Getting out, she dried slowly. She was tired again. Her body was still recuperating, but she could at least move without feeling like she needed a nap every foot or so. She was pulling on a pair of her jeans when someone knocked again. She nearly told him to fuck off when Sandra spoke.

"I've come to see if you need help with the bandage, dear. Ryland said that you were in the shower and I thought you might need some juice as well." She opened the door and smiled. "Oh my, your hair is much longer than I... goodness, it's so lovely."

"It's a pain in the as...butt. I've wanted to cut it all off for years, but every time I got to a barber there was a long line and I didn't want to sit and wait."

Sandra took the brush and asked her to have a seat. She brushed her hair for her and Bronwyn felt stupid, but also loved the feeling of the smooth strokes along her head, which seemed to relax her.

"It's a stylist. For a woman, it's a salon or a stylist. And I wouldn't cut it. It's so beautiful." The strokes were very hypnotic, and she found herself relaxing. "What did you do at the hospital, if you don't mind me asking?"

"I was a nurse." The brush paused then continued. Bronwyn looked at her in the mirror in front of her as Sandra continued. She waited for her to tell her she wasn't smart enough or give her hell for quitting, but she did neither.

"I would imagine that it was difficult to give up. I can't imagine how long it must have taken you to finish med school, then all that time working toward it only to have to it taken from you. I'm sorry for that."

Bronwyn turned, took the brush from her, and stared at her. "Why?" Sandra looked confused at her question. "Why are you being so nice to me? I can't understand any of you. Your sons have been in here twice a day, each of them, and asked how I was feeling. I was offered a laptop to play on and magazines to read. Jules even offered me his reader, telling me if I wanted anything other than what was on there he had a credit. Why? Is it because they think that I'm going to be their brother's mate or something? I'm not."

"Why not?"

Bronwyn started to say that she couldn't answer a question with one when Sandra continued. "Is there something wrong with him? Do you think he'll beat you? Hurt you? Or is it because you've lumped all males together because of a select few?"

"All the men in my life have shit on me." She started to stand when Sandra told her to sit. "I'm not going to be his mate. I don't want to be anyone's mate."

"Has he?" The softly asked question startled her. "Has Ryland shit on you? Has he hurt you? Sold you to that man? Given you to anyone as a plaything?"

"That doesn't mean he won't." She flushed when she realized what she'd said to his mother. "He's bossy and loud. He'll expect me to do his bidding, clean his house, and cook. I won't...I don't know how to do those things."

Bronwyn turned to her when she laughed. It took her a few minutes before she could ask her what the hell she'd found so funny. Bronwyn was ready to have her committed when she finally told her.

"He won't expect you to do any of those things, dear...not unless you want to. He can cook, and is quite good at it. He can clean a bathroom like there's going to be surgery done in there. As for him being bossy and loud? You do all right in that department as well." She stood up and headed for the door. "I have dinner about ready. Come down and eat with us. You'll see that they're animals when there's food involved, but also the most loving men I know."

Bronwyn decided to go down. It was that or stay in that room and go stir crazy. If she was honest with herself, she was bored. And she'd not been bored since...well, she didn't know if she'd ever been bored before. Bronwyn had never been in this part of the house before that she could remember, and followed the sounds to the kitchen. She nearly backed out again when it looked like they were having fun.

"Come here." She was pulled into the room by Ryland, who kissed her on the mouth. She was so shocked by it that she had been handed a handful of silverware and pushed to the dining room before she could think. She was still standing there with it when Neal came in.

"We can use that better if you put it with the plates. Unless this is your plan to keep all the lasagna to yourself." He looked at her oddly. "Are you okay? You look sort of...like someone has hit you."

"He kissed me." He grinned at her and she flushed. "I don't know why he'd do such a thing. Especially in front of...I don't want anyone to get the wrong idea. He's just not going to be my mate. Or me his."

Neal nodded as she started slamming forks and knives onto the table near each place setting. He walked behind her and straightened them. She turned to glare at him when they were halfway around the table.

"You need to vent. I'm just making it neat. Nice trade off, don't you think?"

His grin, she supposed, could be considered charming. She wanted to slug him. "Does that work for you? This charming good-looking bit, does it get you what you want? I don't have anything you want, I promise you." He nodded and took the rest of the silverware away from her. She thought maybe it was a smart move, because she was thinking of using it on him.

"Does this hard ass thing you have going work for you?" She stood there as he finished the table. "The way I see it is this. You're his mate whether you want to be or not. He wants you...well, you've made it clear that you don't want him. Why?"

"I hate that question. A lot of people have asked me that. I don't have an answer. I just can't, that's all." He nodded. "What's that supposed to mean?"

"It means that you can't, not that you won't." She looked at Ryland, who stood in the doorway behind her. "Neal, could you tell Mom that I need a few minutes? I want to talk to Bronwyn." He held out his hand to her. She knew that if she took it something would change, and she was afraid of the kind of change he wanted.

He didn't grab her like she expected him to do when he stepped close to her, but wrapped his arm around her and took her out onto the deck. It was a beautiful night. "I told you I'd show you the kittens." She walked along with him, and wasn't really sure why she was letting him lead her out. "There are seven of them. It's sometimes hard for a human to tell the sex of a kitten at birth, but as a cat myself, I can tell."

He opened the barn door and led her to the back. She was being as quiet as he was, and when he moved to a small area just behind a bale of hay, she looked to where he pointed. The smallest bundles of fur she'd ever seen were all huddled together, and what she thought was their mother was nearby watching them. As soon as she saw Ryland, she purred.

"She knows you." He nodded, sat down, picked up one of the kittens, and lifted it toward her. "I can't. I don't know anything about animals, and less about little tiny ones."

He pulled her down to the hay and sat her onto his lap. Before she could protest or even move off him he cupped her hands around the tiny fur ball. Her heart melted.

"She's beautiful." He looked at her with a smile. "I can't tell them apart either, but she knows what she is. And she wants to be like her mom." She tried to put her back with the others when one of the others brushed against her hand. She picked him up and rubbed him against her cheek.

"Have you ever had a pet before?"

She shook her head and picked up another one. This was a male too. She held them both close to her as she explained. "I wasn't allowed one as a child. My mother said we couldn't afford one. I suppose not if she was using all the money for drugs. Then later, when I was in the foster care system, I couldn't then either. When I got old enough to have one, it was too much trouble, and I didn't know how to care for one anyway." Bronwyn shrugged as she put both kittens down. "It would be hard now, too, with me on the run all the time." She looked at him when he said her name. Bronwyn turned slightly and looked into his eyes. His arousal was right there where she could see it—could feel it under her bottom as a matter of fact—but when she licked her lips, he stared at them as if he wanted to devour them. "Your family is waiting."

Bronwyn didn't recognize her own voice; it was husky and low. "They're going to wonder where we are."

"I don't care." He cupped the back of her head and pulled her to his mouth. He nibbled on her lower lip then suckled it into his mouth. She turned to shove him away, but her fingers and hands had a will of their own and curled around his neck and held him. When he tilted her head and then his she waited for him, wanted him to kiss her. Then his mouth took hers.

There was no gentle build up once he covered her mouth with his, but a conquering. He speared his tongue into her mouth and stroked hers. One of them moaned and it took her seconds to realize it had been her. When he shifted her around so that she was turned to face him she moaned again. His hands were everywhere, gentle and warm. When he lifted his head she was panting as hard as he was, her body on fire, burning for his. He laid his head against her forehead and held her. "Alistair is coming for us. He's whistling so that we'll be warned that he's near." He kissed her quickly on her mouth before he lifted his head. "He didn't want to walk in on something that would scar him and he'd need therapy, he said."

She realized when he started to button her blouse that he'd had her nearly undressed. Slapping his hands away, she quickly put herself together just as he stood up. The barn door opened a second later.

"Mom wants to know if you could come in now. She said everything is ready." He wouldn't look at them, and that embarrassed her more. "Shall I tell her you're coming or that you'll be along soon?"

Bronwyn looked at him, shocked at what he'd said. Stomping toward him when Ryland laughed, she wasn't sure if it was at her or his brother's joke. When she was ready to step into the house, she turned to them both. "Nothing happened. Nothing at all. We were looking at the kittens is all." Alistair nodded. "You can think whatever you want, but nothing happened."

"Sure." Alistair started in and stopped before she could follow. "If nothing happened, then why is your blouse buttoned all walperjawed?"

Ryland laughed harder. She was going to kill them both. Turning around, she fixed her shirt. She was two holes off and it took her two tries before she got it right. She glared at Ryland when he tried to help her again.

"This is your fault." He nodded. "I mean it. If you hadn't tried to undress me and have you…you should just stop trying to get me naked."

He pressed her against the wall and took her mouth again. When he lifted her leg up and put it over his hip, she felt his cock rock into her. He lifted his head and licked along her throat to her shoulder. She grabbed onto his hair and tilted her head to give him more.

"I want you naked right now. I want to bury myself in you and never come out." He rolled into her again; her body felt heavy and needy. "Christ, what I wouldn't give right now to have you in my room, beneath me, riding me. I want you now, Bronwyn."

He turned her away from the door when it opened. She had no idea who had come out, but Ryland growled. It sent a shiver up her body that made her ache. He looked at her when the door closed again.

"We have to go inside." She nodded. "I don't want to. I would rather take you back out to the barn and make love to you. All night. Probably into tomorrow too. But they want us inside."

"We can't…we shouldn't do this."

He shook his head.

"They're going to come for me. I don't want you hurt."

"If you leave me, Bronwyn, it's going to hurt me more than anything they can do to me." He took her hand and they went inside. Dinner was served as soon as they sat down. Christ, she was in big trouble.

CHAPTER 9

Eli Cunningham looked over the lab findings from the day before then tossed them on the desk. It wasn't working. None of it was. And not only that, it was costing more money than he had coming in right now. Making a synthetic drug was not as easy as he'd thought it would be. He glanced at the file he'd been avoiding since he'd had his encounter with Bronwyn. If only the bitch would cooperate, he'd have his money.

He thought about the tigers. He'd been told that all of them had been run off, and that those who hadn't been run off or killed were now a part of another ambush...Crawford's ambush.

But she'd had them. And she protected them as well. One had nearly taken his leg off, and probably would have had he not succeeded in getting the door opened when he had. Christ, that fucker was huge. He leaned back in his chair, and was wondering what to do about them—and her—when Crawford walked in.

"That little bitch you said was hot for me is dead."

Eli looked at him, trying to remember when he'd ever said that to any man before, much less him.

"I think she was just trying to make that boyfriend of hers jealous. He's not anymore."

"You killed them both." Crawford nodded even though it hadn't been a question. "Did you happen to get rid of the bodies this time, or did you leave them to be found by some nosey landlord?"

"Nah, I had them put out at the airport in their car. Somebody will think they were killed there. I even remembered to wipe shit down this time."

Eli looked out the window and counted to ten. How this man had gotten to where he was without someone killing him was mind-boggling. And the fact that he had about fifty cats in his ambush was even more astounding. The man was nothing but a bully, and not even a smart one at that. Eli turned back to him. "When was the last time you made a sweep for cats in this area?" He waited while Crawford pulled out his little notebook. Eli had often wondered if he was actually writing in it or simply drawing pictures because he couldn't read. He waited so long he was ready to rip it out of his hand and read it himself.

"Nearly three months ago. Didn't find much more than a passerby. He's not passing no more...at least passing alive."

Eli started to ask what the hell that meant, but didn't bother. "I had a run in with an ambush of them a week ago. If you had a cell phone worth shit, I could have told you then." Crawford sat up straighter in his chair as Eli continued. "About half a dozen of them. Big fuckers too. And you'll never guess who had control over them."

Crawford looked confused. Eli wanted to hit him. He started to tell him it was a rhetorical question, but didn't want to have to explain that too. Having a brute force was great, but not when the leader was no smarter than the paper he wrote his assignments down on.

"It was Bronwyn Lawrence. She was protecting them, so I would imagine that she can tell you where they are when you find her. You are still looking for her, aren't you?" Crawford nodded. "Well, what's the progress?"

"Progress? Oh, you mean what have I been able to figure out. Why don't you just say that? Any hoo, she isn't in that building no more. It's gone. Somebody went and bulldozed it right to the ground. I went there twice and it's still gone. And that girl friend of hers, she's gone too. I wish you had have given her to me when her mate come up dead. But that man we left in charge there, he said there were laws or some shit."

"Yes, there are laws that he has to follow. It was leave him there in charge or leave you. And you had things to do for me." Eli could hear his IQ lower every minute he spent with this fool. "And I told you to leave her alone. She's our only link to Bronwyn. Once we…. You said she was gone too? When did this happen?"

Crawford shrugged. "Don't know. About a week ago, I guess. Her place is all there like she was coming back, but she hasn't yet. And that guy I had on her, that Otter? He's gone too. I've been looking for him since last week too. You think they being gone together means something?"

Eli laid his head on his desk. A week. She'd been gone a week, which meant that either she was gone in the wind with Bronwyn or she was with the other cat. It was highly unlikely that she had gone to another cat. Her mate from before had been brutal and nasty. He doubted the woman had even been near a man, much less slept with one since.

"You okay there, Eli?" He looked up to see Crawford leaning toward him. "I thought maybe you were upset about Otter. I am. He was a good kid."

Laughing at the absurdity of it all, Eli sat up. He picked up his phone and found his calculator on it. He did some quick math before putting it down again and looking at Crawford.

"You can only spend twenty-five minutes with me a day from now on. And, after you leave, I will need to spend twice that to get even half the brain cells I lost trying to understand you. You're detrimental to my wellbeing." He lifted his hand, already anticipating that he'd have to explain most of the words he'd just used. "Twenty-five minutes. And I'm setting the timer when you come in. Do you have anything else to tell me?"

"I don't think…. You want me to go and check to see if that building is gone still? I could go right there now."

"No. I'm pretty sure that once a building is gone, it's pretty much going to stay that way. But thanks. I want you to find Sindy Wilson. And not to hurt her, just find her and bring her to me. Understand?"

"Yeah. Find Sindy Wilson and bring her to you. I can't hurt her either. I'm betting the others can't hurt her either, right?" Eli said that was correct. "I'll go by her place and see if she's come back. If not, then I'll go to her work place. I have me a friend in there that can tell me what I want."

A friend in the hospital. Eli had visions of his friend being a brain surgeon or something like that. He nodded and, after writing down the instructions in his book, Crawford left.

He was going to have to figure out a better way to run the cats. They were afraid of Crawford; everyone was when he was a cat and pissed, but he was beyond stupid and going to get them killed. How he'd not managed to do that so far was insane. Eli opened the folder with Bronwyn's name on it.

Christ, she was a beauty. Long red hair and eyes that were both scary and hypnotizing at the same time. And her power? He'd never created a more powerful being. And the fact that she could control it was what he wanted...what he needed.

He could make millions from her. Selling her to the military, any military that had the funds he wanted, would do that. Then he'd have the funding that he needed to make him more of a long-term cash flow. Drugs that could do three to four times the damage for half the cost. But he'd charge ten times what he would get for the real stuff.

But he needed her first, and she wasn't doing what he'd wanted her to. Not now, and not when he'd had her the first time. Smiling, he flipped to the back of the folder to see the pictures he'd taken of her the last time.

Eli was a sadist. He knew that, and so did anyone who was caught in his bedroom or the playroom with him for more than five minutes. The only way he could get off was by inflicting physical and psychological pain on his victims, and he loved it. And when he'd had to discipline Bronwyn, he'd come every day just from watching the whip strike her back. Christ, she'd been so good for him. Then she'd gotten away.

Eli tossed the file down. She'd been unconscious when he'd left for the day. Her most recent beating was on a thumb drive to use at home, and her file, the one he had now to go over, was in his brief case. He was just about to shoot his load when his alarm had gone off, telling him that he was needed at the lab. But by the time he'd gotten there the lab was gone. And so was she.

It had taken him nearly a month to figure out that she hadn't been in the place when it went up. The fire marshal had said it was caused by a gas leak that had been filling the building nearly all day. Not likely, since there had been about a dozen cats in the building during that time frame and they would have smelled it. It had been her. She'd gotten loose, and had blown his building and all his work to hell and back.

Just another thing to hold over her head when he found her. And he would too. It was just a matter of time.

Eli picked up his cell when it rang and cringed when he saw it was his ex-wife. There were many other things to do than to listen to her complain about one of his brats again. Eli set the cell down and let her tell her woes to the voicemail. He sent her more money in one month than a small country could use in two years. Eli closed his eyes and was thinking about Bronwyn when he heard the beep that he had new voicemail. Ignoring it, he told himself he'd answer it later. When hell froze over, he'd get back to her. Grinning, he went to find some lunch; then he thought he might go and see if that building was still gone.

~~~

"Do you know what this is?" Keith handed Ryland a picture as he explained where he'd found it. "When we were being shot up by those guys while trying to save Bronwyn, one of the men I was chasing dropped it. I've been working on a recognition program, but it doesn't seem to get it."

Ryland turned it sideways and even upside down, but he didn't know what it was either. It was sort of blurry, but that wasn't it. It seemed to be of a person, but it was hard to tell. He leaned over to Bronwyn and handed it to her. He realized she knew the moment she stood up.

"Where did you get this?" He told her that he'd gotten it from his brother. "I thought that it'd been destroyed. I did it; all of it was gone."

She left the dining room only to return and sit down. She looked around the room and then at Sindy. The two of them were talking, and he wasn't happy to be left out. When he touched her arm she looked at him.

"I need a map."

Nodding, he took her to the office and pulled out one of his dad's county maps. She stood over it with the picture, moving in different directions until she looked at Keith.

"I can't find...is there a way for you to see if there have been any building permits issued in the last...I would say, in the last year? It would be for a big building, a lab." He nodded and she watched him sit at his laptop. "It might be under a different guise. Maybe foods or additives."

"There are two. One is now defunct, called *Better Future*. They had a horrible fire fifteen years ago and...." He looked at her. "You know this one. And one that is under the name of C & C Enterprises. It specializes in enhancement formulas."

She nodded and looked at him. "I'm sure they do. It's the same place. Different name, but the same place. Ryland, I need to talk to you. There's something you should know."

"We all want to know." She looked at Sandra when she spoke. "If it involves you and something that might get you hurt, then I think we all want to know. If Ryland doesn't mind letting us in on it, that is. But you're a part of our family now and—"

"If what I think is going on again is, there might not be a family." Bronwyn looked at Ryland again. "He's experimenting on cats. Not just cats, but all species. When I was there...when he held me captive the last time...he was messing with DNA and shooting it into me. He's trying his best to come up with a super animal that he can sell to a militant force. He doesn't even care who, so long as they have the money."

"And the picture? What is that?" She handed it to him and bent it so that the opposite corners were touching. The picture popped out at him so starkly that he nearly staggered.

"It's special photography programming that was developed for secret shit. It's a mongrel...what he called the

99

ones that didn't make it. He has been trying to make something like me so that he could sell them for cash. It's not his primary goal, but the one he figures is going to make him the most money so that he can focus on his own project. He is trying to come up with a drug that will be lower in cost, but more the punch. He thinks it will be his ticket to being a long term millionaire." She looked around the room. "He is taking big cats. He makes them masturbate until they're dead or their sperm proves to be no longer valid. It's why Crawford is working for him. When he goes in to raze a streak, or as he calls them, an ambush, he takes only the strongest. The children are killed because he doesn't want to wait on them to grow up to use them. It's cheaper, he said, to get the adults for quicker results."

Ryland pulled her onto his lap and, for once, she didn't struggle. He needed to think. This was beyond what he'd thought the man wanted her for. He knew he probably wanted her for breeding purposes, but not like this. He pulled her tighter against him as he asked questions.

"You destroyed the first lab then?" She nodded. "I'm assuming that you thought it was over and that he was done. Because when the lab went up, everything went with it."

"Yes. And it wasn't easy to do for me either. There were a few animals there. Most of them were beyond…. Those that could speak begged me to leave them. They'd been abused so horribly that it was hard to tell what they were any longer. And the few that could leave, they're now hidden away."

"I've been helping her find them places." Sindy spoke for the first time. "Some of them, about five, went to another country after I was able to get them to a point where they could move. The rest, the ones that couldn't travel far, have new identities and jobs that suit their new lifestyles."

"Mrs. Wentmore, the lady at the library. She's one of them, isn't she?" Bronwyn and Sindy both nodded at his mom's question. "Oh my goodness. That poor woman. She told me that she'd been in an automobile accident."

"She thinks she was." Bronwyn pulled away and started pacing. "All of them think that they were in an automobile accident of some sort. I didn't want them to ever think about it again, so I helped them."

"She also gave them a new outlook on life. Had them think about how lucky they'd been, and that they were going to live their lives to the fullest." Sindy smiled sadly at him. "Bronwyn said that no one should remember that place, just her."

Ryland stood up and went to her. When she backed up he took her to him anyway, the need to hold her more overwhelming than her need to run. He had to help her; he would. Looking around the room again, he spoke to all of them.

"We'll need as much information as we can get on the lab and anything that we can get on the comings and goings. Keith, see if you can find anything on Cunningham. No first name, but that shouldn't be too hard for you. Alistair, see what you can figure out about Crawford and his mercenaries. There has to be something on them somewhere. Mom has some old newspapers that might help." He lifted Bronwyn's chin up and looked down at her. "You're going to give us as much information as you can on the old lab. People's names if you knew them, some of the tigers or other weres if you know them as well."

"I want to help." Sindy flushed. "I can help. I'm not working now, so I would like something to keep me busy. I've never been idle before."

"Good. I have a project that I want you to work on that has nothing to do with this one." At her crestfallen face, he smiled. "Don't worry, you'll be plenty busy. I want you to set up a clinic for us. A place where we can go without fear of being found out. And if the shit hits the fan like I think it's going to, then we might have need of it sooner rather than later."

"I can do that. I would love to do that." She laughed. "I'll even put in some supplies for babies that might be coming around soon too."

She went away laughing, and Ryland looked at Bronwyn. She had the most terrified look on her face. Before she could say whatever was on the tip of her tongue, he kissed her. Hard and fast, he pulled her to him so there was no doubt to her that he, too, was excited about the thought of babies being born.

CHAPTER 10

Bronwyn was in the bathroom when she heard the door open. Not bothering to look, she figured it was Sindy as she said she'd bring her some of her clothes to put on. Bronwyn knew she was going to have to go out soon and get some. She was seriously tired of the two shirts she was wearing all the time. When she came out she was just going to ask Sindy which web sites to shop from when she saw who was there.

"Sindy said to give you these." She took the shirt and panties from Ryland. "She said to tell you she'd see you in the morning. She was downloading something."

Nodding, she pulled the clothes to her chest. "What are you doing in here? I thought that this is where your mom said I could stay now."

"It is. It's my old room." He toed off his shoes and then started on the buttons of his shirt. "I have to go to the office tomorrow. Would you like to come with me? We can stop by some shops if you need something."

"I do." She tossed the clothes on the bed and put her hands on her hips. "What are you doing? You can't think you're sleeping in here. With me."

"I do. Though I doubt we'll be getting much in the way of sleep." The shirt came off and he wore a white t-shirt under it.

It was tight and molded to his muscles like it had been painted on him. She could see the tufts of hair peeking up from the top. When he reached for his belt she moved toward the door. There was no way she was sleeping with this arrogant ass, no matter how sexy he was. He stepped in front of her before she got there.

"I'm going to find another room. Maybe I can bunk with Sindy." He shook his head and pulled her toward him. "Ryland, this isn't going to happen."

He molded her body to his and she felt that not only did he look muscled, she could now feel them. All of them. And his mouth was wonderfully warm and wet against her throat. She tried again to tell him she wasn't sleeping with him.

"Okay. But I can do this to you, can't I?"

She wanted to beg him not to stop, but he was moving his mouth along her throat to just behind her ear.

"And this. You have the most wonderful taste. Like strawberries. No, that's not quite right, more like wet, warm strawberries."

"Ryland, you can't do any of that." Her hands moved to curl into his hair to jerk him away, but when they got there he nipped at her tender flesh and held on. "Please stop now. This is only going to get us into trouble."

"Christ, I certainly hope so." He lifted her up and she wrapped her legs around him. He cupped her ass tight, pulling her over him until she was riding him. The wall behind her felt wonderful and supportive. As soon as she moaned he tore her shirt from her.

"I don't have any more clothes." She thought he said good, but wasn't sure as he took her breast into his mouth through her bra. Everything seemed to fade away. It was just him and her, and she wanted it all.

She heard her bra tear and moaned. She really was going to be without anything to wear if he kept this up. When he pushed her legs down from his hips and stepped back, she reached for him. But before she could pull him back to her he dropped to his knees in front of her.

"I want to eat you." Her pants were ripped down both sides and he tossed them away. "Christ, you smell delicious. I want to eat you as you come."

She was panting so hard she was dizzy. Her body was tight with need for him, of what she knew deep within her only he could give her. While she watched him he slid his hands under her panties, the only barrier left between his mouth and her, and tore them from her body.

He ran his hands up and down her thighs, watching her as he did so. She trembled, and he smiled at her as he spread her legs wider for him. He moved slowly toward her, and she knew that the moment he touched her she was going to come. She held her breath. His tongue darted out and teased her: her breath hitched.

"Ryland, please stop this teasing and take me." He grinned and told her to beg. "I'm begging you. I'm pleading with you, please give me release."

"When I do, I'm going to finish. There won't be any going back after tonight. You know as well as I do that this thing between us won't be denied."

She looked away, afraid.

"Bronwyn, I won't ever hurt you. Not ever. I'm falling in love with you."

"He'll come for you. The moment he knows that he can get to me through you, he'll come for you too."

"Let him. I'm more than ready for his fucking ass." He leaned in, took her clit into his mouth, and sucked. She screamed out his name as her climax consumed her. And he didn't stop, didn't slow as he brought her to peak over and over. She was weak with it when he finally sat back again.

Moving up her body, he nipped at her flesh; never to the point of real pain, but enough to know that he wanted her to be marked by him. When he made it to her navel he swirled his tongue there, suckling at the flesh until she had to hold on to him or fall. Begging him now, for what she had no idea, he stood up and took her nipple deep into his mouth as he pulled his snap and zipper out of his pants, freeing his cock.

He was thick with need and a stream of his cum dripped from the end. She wanted to drink from him, take him into her mouth, feel him come down her throat, but he stopped her by wrapping his hand around hers.

"Too close. You touch me anymore and I'll spill all over you. I need to be inside of you." He guided her to the bed and, when it touched the backs of her calves, she felt him lift her, his mouth doing incredible things to her breasts the entire time.

When she was laying back, his body over hers, she looked up at him. His cat, the beast deep within him, seemed to stare back at her. She touched her fingers to his cheek and she saw him snarl.

"He wants you." She nodded. "Are you giving him permission to take you? He wants me to claim you for both of us."

His cock nudged at her entrance. She felt her pussy gush more cream for him. She was hurting; her need was too tightly coiled in her. When he asked her again, the thick head of his cock moved into her. She arched up and her body tumbled over the edge. She screamed out her consent.

He snarled at her and she tilted her neck, giving him what no other man would ever touch. As soon as he slammed into her to his hilt he sank his teeth into her shoulder. She held him to her, wrapped her legs around him as he took her, hard, deep strokes that she felt at the back of her throat. When he stiffened, his body arched up and she looked at him.

Blood dripped from his mouth and chin; his eyes had lightened, changed to his cat as he filled her. Screaming out again, she clutched him hard enough that her nails drew blood at his chest and she came again. When he pressed her mouth to his wounds she instinctively licked, then covered her mouth over them and suckled. He roared this time. His cat moved along his body so that she saw him; fur replaced skin then back again. Stripes marred his flesh then were gone. His cat claimed her even as she drank from him. When he fell over her, his body spent, she felt the room shift, the lights dim then brighten. Suddenly, it was too much and she closed her eyes just as he rolled to the side and took her with him.

The last thing she heard before exhaustion took her was him telling her that he loved her. That he loved her for all time and that she was his. She wanted to be pissed. Wanted to tell him that she belonged to no one, but it felt right. It felt true. She was his mate.

~~~

Ryland was standing in the kitchen when his mom came down. He flushed when she smiled at him. He knew that she could smell that they'd bonded. There wasn't a cat alive that wouldn't be able to tell that. She moved to the stove while he drank the last of his tea.

"She's going into town with me. She needs some things." His mom nodded. "I bought a house."

She looked at him and laughed. "Well, you wasted no time, did you? Have you told Bronwyn yet?"

"I'm going to take her there today. I've not seen it either. We might…I was thinking we might stay in town tonight, get things squared away for us to move in when things are settled." She smiled at him and nodded. "She and I are mates."

"We heard."

He flushed again, remembering that she'd screamed and that, when he'd taken her, he'd roared.

"You'll need your own home if you're going to be mates."

He laughed. His mother was politely telling him that they needed their own place if they were going to be that noisy. He kissed her on the cheek and looked to the door when it opened. Bronwyn stood there.

"Hi." He'd made love with her again before coming downstairs. She'd told him that she needed to shower, and that doing it alone would be much quicker if he wanted to get to his job. He'd been tempted, very much so, to say fuck it and stay in bed with her all day. But they both had things they needed to do.

"Hi. I had to borrow one of your shirts." She pulled it away from her front. "I don't have a lot to wear here. Not that I did anyway, but this is…. I babble when I'm nervous."

"Why are you nervous?" His mom asked her to sit as she continued talking. "I was just talking to Ryland. He said that you're going to get a few things to wear, so that'll be nice. There's a lovely shop on Seventh Street. It's only a block or two from the Towers."

"I think that's a little out of my price range." Bronwyn smiled at his mom when she set a plate of ham and muffins in front of her. "I have to collect some things from a few places. Money mostly. I couldn't open a bank account so I stashed cash when I had it."

"Because that man was chasing you." She nodded at his statement. "Well, he knows you're here now, but it wouldn't matter. I have enough money for whatever you need." He knew the moment it left his mouth it had been wrong. She stiffened, and his mother left the room with a pat on his back. He raised his hands to have her stop before she exploded, but she wasn't having it.

"You think because we fucked that I'm going to take your money?" He shook his head, but before he could explain, she punched her finger into his chest. "You think that last night gives you the right to make me a kept woman? That you owe me, or worse yet, own me?"

"No, I only meant—"

"Only meant what? That I'm poor and helpless, and need a big, bad-assed tiger to make me safe and secure? I'll have you know that I'm quite capable of taking care of myself. I've been doing it a very long time and I'm fucking good at it. And if I—"

He kissed her. It worked well enough to shut her up, but now he wanted to take her back upstairs and make love to her again. When she wrapped her arms around him he pressed her against the closest hard surface he could find. The refrigerator was perfect. When her legs came up and wrapped around him he rocked into her and she moaned.

"You're a pain in the ass, did you know that?" He laughed when she nodded. "If this was our home, I'd think nothing of taking you right here and right now, but there are a lot of people in this house who need to eat. Mom is holding them off right now."

She looked to the door then back at him. "Aren't you a bad ass male? Make them go away for thirty minutes. We'll make it a quickie."

He set her on the counter and stepped back. "We have to go. And we have to talk about your short fuse. I wasn't saying I owned you, but that you own me…lock, stock, and all my money. I meant that since I ripped them off you, I'll gladly replace them. And besides, I love seeing you in my clothes."

He reached for the last muffin and tossed it at her as the door opened and his family spilled in. He nodded to all five of his brothers and his mom. He helped her off the counter and looked at his family. "I know that each of you have had contact with Bronwyn over the past weeks, but I want to take this time to formally introduce you to my mate. Bronwyn Lawrence, this is my family. Alistair is my partner at the Towers, as is Neal, and Brock is my enforcer, or the heavy. This is Jules, he's the owner of a pottery company downtown that does stoneware and some art stuff, and this is Keith. Keith is our nerd. If he can't fix it, then you should simply replace it. It won't be fixable."

"And I'm his mom, Sandra Golden." His mom hugged her. "Welcome to the family, dear. You're going to be a wonderful addition."

He took her out to the car and, when he got in the limo after her, she moved to the other side of the seat and looked at him. He waited. When they had left he knew that something had happened, something about his family, but he didn't know what. He knew that if he were in her shoes, he'd have been overwhelmed.

"I don't want them to get hurt." She took a deep breath. "None of them. But they will. You know that, right?"

"I know that the person we're dealing with is a monster, and we've not had a great deal of experience with men like him. I know that, especially after I saw him work to get you the other day, he'll stop at nothing, not even killing anyone to get you." She nodded. "But I'm not a kind and generous man when it comes to them, my family, and you. You're my mate, my love. I will die before he gets his hands on you."

She looked out the window and stayed where she was. "I was going to leave last night. Sindy was safe, and I knew that no matter how pissed you might have been at me you would keep her safe. But I couldn't."

She looked at him. There were tears there and he wanted to wipe them away and hold her, but she shook her head when he started to move. He wanted to tell her that he loved her and that he would have found her because of their blood connection now, but that wasn't what she wanted or needed to hear. He reached for her hand instead.

"I'm glad you didn't leave me. I don't know what I would have done if you had." He grinned at her. "I bought you something. Something you've never had before and, if you had left, then I would have had to deal with all the stuff that comes from it on my own."

She looked at him suspiciously. "What the hell have you done? Please tell me that you didn't order me clothes. Ryland, I don't do fancy. I like my jeans and t-shirts. I don't like people, and I'm not what one would call socially active."

He laughed. He kissed her hand then pulled her to him. She was sitting in his lap when the limo stopped. He'd asked the driver to take them to the new house first. If there were any changes they needed to make before they moved in he could get started on them this morning. When the door opened he held her tight and told her what he'd done.

"It's ours. I know it looks big, but…." She looked at him then at the open door. "I bought us a house."

"You didn't." He nodded. "When? During sex or while I was in the shower? Either way, it was fucking fast."

"No, I bought it before all that. I had a deal with my mom. If I didn't buy a house she would do it for me. She was tired of me living in a hotel. I wasn't going to do it at all, then I met you. Then I needed one with you." He slipped from under her, got out, and reached for her. "Come on. You can be pissed with me after we see it."

"You've never even seen it?" she asked from within the depths of the limo. He told her he hadn't. When she took his hand he thought for sure he heard her call him a moronic idiot, but wasn't sure. When they turned to look at their new house, he fell in love with it and she seemed awestruck.

"Holy monkey feather, it's fucking huge." She looked at him, smiling. "Maybe I will let you buy me clothes."

She liked it. That's all he could think as they walked up the front steps. She really liked it. As soon as they stepped into the main entrance, the realtor greeted them. Ryland took the keys and handed them to Bronwyn. "For you." Then he bent on one knee and pulled out his mother's engagement ring that Sandra had given him just before they left. "Bronwyn Lawrence, will you marry me so that I can live here with you for the rest of our lives?"

"Get up, you idiot. I said I wasn't leaving you." He held her hand. "You're for serious?"

"Yes. Now you say yes so I can get up and kiss you properly." She looked scared and he stood up. "I love you. Say yes."

"Yes, but there are things you have to know about me that might—"

She said yes. He pulled her to him and kissed her, devoured her, and moved them to the wall, where she wrapped her legs around him. This could be habit forming. When someone cleared their throat behind them, he turned. The fucking agent. He looked back at Bronwyn.

"We have company. Maybe we should just look around some other time when we can take our time." She nodded as she dropped her feet to the floor. "We're going to buy us a bed first."

Laughing, they thanked the real-estate agent and left for his office. By the time they got there, he'd made arrangements to have the best security system put into place and for a service to have an armed guard at the front gates. He was mated and a homeowner. He was the happiest he'd been in his life.

CHAPTER 11

Bronwyn looked over the catalogues she'd been handed and sat at his front desk. Between answering the phone and taking people in and out of his office she tried to find some clothes. It wasn't working. She was more of a discount shopper, and this thing she'd been handed had stuff in it that she'd never wear to anything. She tossed it in the trash.

"No much of a shopper, huh?"

She looked up at the woman she'd never seen before.

"I hate it too. Sort of like looking at a magazine that specializes in naked men. Just not the same."

"If you say so." Bronwyn reached out and touched her mind. Cat, tiger, and one that belonged to Crawford. Bronwyn leaned back in the chair as she reached for Brock. He was close, and she had learned that he was also head of security. She told him what was going on, to come to her on a ruse.

"I'm Angela Marcus. I'm here to see the male." She reached out her hand and Bronwyn ignored it. "You're not very friendly, are you?"

"Nope. Sit down." The cat had no choice in the matter as Bronwyn was more powerful and was mate to the male in the other room. She reached for him. *Come here now. Be aggressive.*

She had no idea that he would be so quick. So when Brock came around the corner shifting into a cat, and the door opened behind her and Ryland was one too, she tried not to be startled.

"You were saying something about needing to talk to the male. Here he is. Speak."

The girl cowered then dropped to her knees. Terror poured from her as she lay supine on the carpet. "He sent me to tell the male that he is required to report to him by noon tomorrow. He said that he will be coming for his ambush, and felt it only fair that he gave you fair warning, as he knows that your mother is in house. He wants the two women. The ones that he harbors."

Bronwyn looked at Ryland. "She's telling the truth. She's going to be beaten if she comes back without an answer from you. You should also know that she's been raped repeatedly and beaten regularly because she's a lesser female."

Hold her here. Can she contact her male?

She told him that she'd taken care of her ability to contact anyone through any kind of link when she'd figured out she was a cat.

I'm going to shift back to talk to her, and would rather not do that naked.

Good. I'll watch her. She winked at Brock. *Behave before I tell Ryland that you're flirting with me.*

Ryland growled as he walked back into his office. A few minutes later he came out putting on a tie, not the one he'd come in with that morning. He kissed her on the nose and looked at the female on the floor.

"Could you please sit in the chair? I'd like a few words with you." She didn't move for several seconds, then looked up at him. "Please. I'm not going to kill the messenger."

"You want me to have a seat? On a chair?"

Ryland nodded then looked at her.

Bronwyn wanted to tell him the girl was confused by him being nice to her, but she thought he got it.

When the girl sat down she didn't look up. Sindy had been much the same way when she'd first been mated to Dana…wouldn't look at anyone or have an opinion on anything. It had been terrifying for Bronwyn to see her friend so beaten.

"Who is your male, and how did you come to be with him?" She would have to answer. Ryland was a male, he required respect, and truth was one of the things he would get. Just not all of it…not if he didn't ask the right questions.

"When did he take your streak?"

She looked from Bronwyn, to Ryland, then back down.

"You will answer."

"Six months ago. He came to our streak the day before, saying that he wanted to see if he could get some ideas for his own. He's…the male, my lady, he's not at all smart."

Ryland sat on the edge of her desk and spoke to her through their link. *You've done this before, so ask her what we need to know so that we have an advantage over the idiot. Is he really not smart?*

He's stupid. And I don't mean in just the leading sort of way. He's really stupid. She looked at him. *You don't mind me doing this?*

He kissed her nose again and told her to go for it. She nodded then looked at him again. *She can't go back. Crawford fully expects you to kill her for this, as does she. If she does go back, he'll think she failed and kill her anyway. She'll need safe passage. I can offer her that. I have a system in place, but it will have to be as soon as we're finished. I don't have any cash to—*

You get the information we need and I'll make sure she's funded. But promise me something.

She nodded.

Please let me help you when you do that from now on. I want to help, and I'll feel better if you let me help, too.

She nodded and turned to the girl. It took her over an hour to get what they needed, and in the end, the girl was sobbing out her story. She had been raped by the entire ambush, what Crawford called his ten or so men. The razing had left her entire family dead, as well as all the other children in the group and all the men that weren't strong enough to fight them for more than five minutes.

Brock had gone back to his office to dress. Bronwyn found out that everyone that worked there had several changes of clothes in their offices in the event something like this happened. This was the first time for both of them. He came back and took the girl to the cafeteria, and then he was going to take her to a point, a place Bronwyn had set up for her while they were eating. There she would be taken to another streak, then moved on from there until she was far away. Her ability to be contacted or to make contact with Crawford had been severed.

Bronwyn followed Ryland into his office.

"She is starved. Do you suppose he does that to all of the people he takes?"

She nodded.

"There should be someone making him pay for what he's doing instead of allowing it to happen all this time. What do you suppose him and Cunningham get out of treating them this way?"

She stood up to pace. This was one of the things she had to tell him, something that she'd found out from Sindy and now from this girl. She started bluntly. She wasn't much for beating around the bush.

"He keeps the younger females because they make excellent whores for him and his men. They're fed better, but only marginally. The older females are used in the kitchens and on any other projects that he has them do. He's even farmed them out as house servants to other larger males. There they are raped when the mood strikes the male and, when they fight back or do something wrong, they're killed." She looked at him. "I can read their minds. I can see their every thought, their every memory, but I can't you...not you or Alistair. I don't know why because I can speak to you both, but I can't read you."

"That's how you know what's going on all the time. How you knew that she was here to cause problems instead of just coming to the office with an appointment." She nodded. "Okay. That's helpful to know. But why do you suppose you can't read Alistair and me?"

"You're not pissed about this? About me being able to read her mind? You can't possibly be okay with this." She looked at him and frowned. "You're not like anyone I've ever encountered before."

He laughed. "Good. I'll keep you on your toes. But your ability to read minds? I had already figured that out. When those animals came to the building to get you I remembered how you simply knew where they were aiming their guns. You seemed to be one step ahead of them all the time. Thankfully, because I doubt we would have survived had you not been."

"I don't understand you." He laughed again. "You keep...I think you're going to react one way and you do something else. You're not like other males I've met. Neither human nor other species."

"I want to be different. I want to be…my father was like you said. You would have liked him, I think. And he would have adored you. He was a man who didn't wait for committees to make decisions. He did what he said felt right in his gut. He was well respected when he died. And well loved. I'll never be able to fill his shoes. He was a great man."

She went to him and crawled into his lap. "You're a great man too. You drive me crazy, but you're a great man."

"Thank you." The phone rang and she started to get up. "I turned the service on. How about if I get through this last bit of paperwork then we get to shopping? I take it you didn't order anything online." She told him no. "Good. I want to watch you try things on, and then know just how to remove them later from your luscious body."

~~~

She wasn't a good shopper, but he was having a blast making her try things on. Every time she looked at the jeans and shirts, he would bring her to something much softer and feminine. She hated him for it. Laughing when she came out of the dressing room with something he'd asked her to try on, she had put the dress on backwards and had pulled on her tennis shoes.

Walking up behind her in the three-way mirror, he studied her. When he was behind her again, he sent the woman helping them away. He wanted her all to himself for a little while.

"I like this one very much." He peeled it off her shoulders to her waist, trapping her arms. "Especially how easy it is to get to you when you wear it like this. Especially like this."

He cupped her breast and pulled her back against him. He had a perfect view of her in the mirrors as he unsnapped her bra and filled his palms with her breasts. They were heavy and full, her nipples hard and pink. Pinching them between his thumb and finger, he rolled them until she moaned.

"I want to take you, right here right now." She moaned and he rocked into her ass. "Lean over the couch in front of you. I'm going to do this fast and dirty. I promise to make it up to you later."

She moved forward out of his grasp and did as he requested, taking the dress off completely as she moved. Opening her legs, she looked over her shoulder at him. Christ, he was going to enjoy this. Moving up behind her he reached for the clerk, another cat friend of his family, and told her to lock up and go to her office. He tore Bronwyn's panties off her even as he heard the lock click into place.

Reaching around to her pussy, he felt that she was wet and gathered her cream on his finger. They watched each other as he took his soaking finger to his mouth and licked it clean. She moved her ass back against him and he groaned.

"You'll have to try not to scream. I love that you do; your screaming out my name makes me come all that much harder." He opened his pants, not bothering to take them off, and lifted his shirt out of his way. "I'm not going to last long. Watching my cock go in and out of you like this is going to be delicious."

"Please fuck me, Ryland. I want to feel your—Christ, yes." He entered her hard and grabbed her hips. She moved back against him every time he pulled back. Holding her as still as he could, he leaned over her and took her to the couch, her head resting on it as he fucked her.

Ryland wanted to bite her desperately, but he knew that if he did he'd roar, and this was neither the time nor the place to have him doing that. He reached between her thighs, ran his fingers though her cream again, and pressed against her clit.

121

"Come for me, Bronwyn. Come so I can join you when you tighten around my cock." She put her hand in her mouth and screamed. Her release was so powerful that she nearly bucked him off. Pinching her clit again, he came with her. His body felt his climax from the tip of his toes to his head. He held her down while he licked along her shoulder.

"Do it. Bite me. I want to feel your teeth sink into me and make me come again."

He couldn't stop his canines at they dropped and he bit her. This time when she came she screamed, but not loudly. He fucked her through that climax and another as her body reacted to him licking the wound closed. He held her that way, under him, both of their heads on the couch, until he could move again.

"We've ruined this dress." He looked at the mess under his feet and grinned at her. "If you think I'm wearing that thing again then you're nuttier than I first thought."

"What if I wanted you to wear it like you just did? Would you wear it just for me?" Her eyes darkened and he had his answer. "We'll take it with us so we don't have to explain what happened to it."

They were on the way to another shop, this one for furniture, thirty minutes later. He had the clerk send over ten pair of varying types of jeans and t-shirts in her size as well. Everything was going to his hotel room, where they would sort things out.

They went to an antique store to get some things. She wandered around the place, not touching anything, and he walked up behind her after telling the cashier they would look around and find him if they found anything they liked. He wrapped his hands around her waist.

"They have memories too." It took him a second or two to realize what she meant. "Not many sad ones, but a few. Would it be alright if I said no even if it was a lovely piece?"

"Yes. Of course. I never thought of you being able to feel that sort of thing. I'm sorry. If you'd rather go to a new store, we can—"

"Sir. I'm sorry. I just heard that you and your lovely bride-to-be were in the store. Let me show you around."

Bronwyn looked at him and smiled.

"Oh my, Tommy said you were a beauty, but you're more than that, aren't you?"

They were shown some of his better pieces, he said. Ryland was looking at a desk that he thought would be nice in his home office. He was about to make an offer on it when the owner and Bronwyn came up behind him.

He's a crook.

He turned fully to look at her.

Some of these things he's stolen, and a few that he didn't are in such ill repair that if you got them home, they'd fall apart the first time you used them. The only nice pieces he has are in his own office. And I want that desk.

He grinned at her. "You want it, you'll have it." She shook her head and he stepped back. This was going to be fun, he just knew it.

She looked at the owner. "You do know that you're the only antique in this room, don't you?" He looked ready to deny it and she smiled again. "Lie to me and I'll shoot you in the foot."

He noticed then that her gun was at her thigh. "Miss, perhaps you should go to another establishment. I don't like to be accused falsely in my own store."

"Then we can step outside for all I give a shit. This desk here is a fake. You made it look old by buying some stain and putting it on sloppily. And the second my mate throws me onto it to have some fun, it would likely kill us both." She reached over, shook it hard, and it groaned. "And don't even try to tell me it's oak. Its pine and we both know it." She handed Ryland her gun and hopped up on the desk in question. It fell under her weight. She looked at the broken mess, picked up a board, and handed it to the owner. He moved back from her.

"You are going to sell us that desk in your office. And you're going to have it delivered to our new home today. Understand me?" He started to sputter. "I'm this close to calling my uncle Gusto and telling him about you."

"Gusto Macneary of Macneary Services is your uncle?" She didn't move, but the owner started nodding. "You'll get it today. I'll have it cleaned out at once. There is a lovely lamp that I picked up for a song that I'll throw in as well." He walked away yelling for his assistant.

"Who's Macneary?"

She shrugged and walked to the door. He followed behind her, laughing, after giving the owner the address of their house. He found her on the street walking toward another shop.

"He was there in his mind. He won't call him, but he is afraid that I will. He's something of a thug and this guy hates him. He's afraid of him too. I don't think we have anything to worry about. The desk will be delivered, and the nice little lamp he picked up for a song too."

He laughed, roared with it. She was priceless and all his. As he wrapped his arm around her waist and held her to him, he told her that he was taking her to his next negotiations meeting. She would be his secret weapon.

"I can do that. I can let you know what each person is thinking about you. If there are any thoughts about your body, however, all bets are off and I'm going to hurt someone."

They bought a bedroom suite and a mattress and linens. They thought about getting more, but as they'd neither one seen the inside of the house, they opted to wait. And they would be back to this store. Everyone, she said, was polite and honest.

CHAPTER 12

"Where is she?" Eli had gotten the call in the middle of the night, and was just now awake enough to understand what Crawford was telling him. He'd found one of the women. He just wasn't sure which.

"I sent me a mercenary. You know, one of those people you're always sending out to talk to people first? Well, I sent me one to the cat's office. Before I could get much outta her, I thought she was killed. Only thing is she said that Bronwyn was there." He laughed. "Damned if that ain't the shit."

"Yes, the shit, and it's emissary, not a mercenary. You're a mercenary and an...never mind. Where is she now? Your...mercenary?" Christ, this man was killing him. "Can I please speak to her?"

"I don't know where she's at."

Eli waited. Closing his eyes, he counted to ten. Then twenty. The man was simply going to die a slow and painful death, and soon. "What do you mean you don't know where she's at?" He spoke each work precisely and hard so there was no way he'd mistake that he was pissed. "How did you find out this information if you didn't talk to her?"

"'Cause I can hear her thinking just like she can me." That would be a trip he'd never take, but waited as he continued. "We have that thing you're always saying that Bronwyn has. Where we can talk to her. You know, not being in the same—"

"I understand now." Eli looked at the clock. "It's four in the morning. Why are you just now calling me?"

"She was gone. I keep telling you stuff and you don't listen to me. She. Is. Gone. Shit." He heard someone else speaking and then Crawford laughed. "Mikey wants to know if you was sleeping?"

Eli put his finger to his head and pretended to blow his brains out. This wasn't the kind of start to his day he wanted, yet it was nothing out of the ordinary for him and Crawford to have these sorts of conversations. He opened his eyes and turned on the light. "What building did you find the cats in? And without going into a great deal of unnecessary information, tell me why you can't find the girl."

There was a pause and Eli knew that he was thinking about each word so that he'd give him what he wanted. The moron had to know that he was at the end of his patience and tolerance for him.

"He is at the Golden Towers. But I don't got a name. She just said that she could smell 'em and that she was going to find them. And can't find the girl?" There was another pause and conversation close before he answered. "Her connection, the thing that I can talk to her with, it's gone. Mikey said to say it was like she just disappeared."

Mikey was getting a fucking medal. Eli pulled up a search on the Golden Towers. He read through it quickly and found that the owner, Ryland Golden, was a billionaire, and that he was in the line to make a great deal more if the deal he had been working on came through. He glanced at the date. A month ago, so it was plausible that he was worth more now. He leaned back in his chair. "I'll go and see Mr. Golden myself. I don't know how to find out who his cats are in the building, but I will see if I can find Bronwyn. She probably works in one of the lower offices as a mail clerk or something."

Eli didn't have the same feelings for females that Crawford did, but he knew that no one would put Bronwyn at a desk without her killing someone. She was volatile and mean. He glanced at the scar on his right hand that she'd given him once when he'd offered to shake her hand. Of course she'd been chained up and had been beaten beforehand, but he wanted her to feel that she could trust him. She hadn't, and he'd paid. Well, so had she, but that was later.

"I'm going to get his ambush, though. He can't be walking around acting like he's the shit and all."

Eli started to ask him what his obsession with shit was, but knew that he'd have to explain the word "obsession" to him and it just wasn't worth it.

"Yes, you can take his whatever. In the meantime, I want you to go to the lab and scare me up some more workers. Not kill them, scare them. I want them to be able to do the everyday things without bleeding or needing a wheelchair. Understand?"

"Yeah, I got you. Just get some humans and take them to the lab."

Eli hung up before he could ask any more questions. He had a pounding headache and it was barely four-thirty in the morning. He looked over the article on Golden. He was in his late thirties and never married. He had several brothers, it said, and two of them worked with him at the Towers. It also said that he had a mother who had also worked there, but she had retired some years ago. This man sounded like someone he could get to like...a man who knew the value of money and who had lots of it. Eli went to the bathroom to get ready for the day, knowing that he'd never get back to sleep.

He worked until just after nine and called Ryland's secretary to make an appointment with Golden. He was put on hold and, when she came back, she said that Mr. Golden didn't have any openings until the end of the week, and would he like to set it up?

"End of the week? It's only Monday. He can't slide in someone who might have a business deal for him? One that would make him double what he has now?" She said that he did not. "Yeah, make it for the early part of the day. I have things to do as well."

She told him ten on Friday and that he would be allotted thirty minutes. He nearly told her to forget it, but agreed. He didn't have any deal except for trying to get him to give him Bronwyn, but he did want to size up the man. He might be a welcome adversary some day.

But that wouldn't mean that he'd stop looking for Bronwyn. He decided that he'd go to the Towers and see if he noticed her coming in or out. If he could snatch her before Friday then that would be good too. If not, then he'd get into the building and search for her. He wasn't sure how he'd do that yet, but he'd think of something. He did his best thinking when he was under pressure.

~~~

The hotel was lovely. She walked around touching things without really seeing them. When he came up behind her, she leaned back into his chest. They were just waiting on breakfast before they went to his office, then to the house. She was actually looking forward to seeing the house.

They'd looked at the realtor's pictures they'd been given. The house really was huge, and had such a big backyard that she wanted to walk around in her bare feet. There was also a pool and a little house on the property, as well as a five-car garage with an apartment over it. She asked him why and he said that whoever cooked for them would live there.

"But we don't need a cook if you'd rather do it. My mom did it for us all these years." She shrugged and told him she didn't have the first clue about cooking. "Then you might need some help with the house. And I want you relaxed all the time so that when I come home from work I can relax inside of you."

They'd made love when they got to the hotel, then in the shower, and after dinner. She told him that she was tired and that she needed to rest. Actually, she was a little sore; he seemed to know it and pampered her the rest of the evening. She had felt amazingly loved and decadent.

His cell phone rang before she could tell him she could relax him now. She knew the moment he tightened his grip on her that it was bad. She held still and listened to him speak.

"When did he call? Yes, that's good. Friday is good. No, it's fine. I'm sorry, he's not anyone I would want to meet alone, so you were right to check with Brock's secretary first on the time. Thank you, I'll be in soon." He put the phone back in his pocket. "Cunningham just called my office to set up a time to see me. He told the switchboard operator that he had a deal for me that would double my worth."

"He's talking about me." He nodded. "That means that he knows that I was there somehow. Maybe Angela contacted him before she spoke to me. But I didn't see a cell phone on her."

His phone rang again before he had a chance to answer her. This time he was pissed right away; his cat appeared twice before he hung up. He took several deep breaths before he said anything to her, and she waited. She knew what it was like to have a temper that could get the better of you.

"I think that was the moron who raises streaks, Forest Crawford." He looked at her with a half grin. "He seems to think that I'm going to be pleasantly surprised when he comes to visit my home. I wonder how he thinks having anything to do with him will be any sort of pleasure."

"How did he know how to find you? I mean, you haven't taken out an ad or anything, have you?" She was half kidding, and when he nodded, she asked him what he meant.

"We have to register to any place that we move to. I haven't taken it very seriously, but I did put my name down about five years ago when they started cracking down more. It was required of all paranormals to have a sort of record of us. I never gave them anything but my cell phone number, so I don't know where he got my address."

"He tell you where you lived or did he ask you?"

He shook his head.

"Then he's bluffing. Or he knows where your family is living. Your mom, is she on this registry too?"

He nodded, suddenly afraid. She could see it on his face. "She would have filed that Dad passed away and that I was the male now. She would more than likely have filled out all the information they asked of her."

"Your mom is very resourceful. I would bet any amount of money that he has no more information on her than he does on you. She has a post office box she told me she uses for things she doesn't care about but needs an address for. She said she checks it about once a month if she's mailing something." She had told her yesterday when they'd been talking about spam. "She's not going to be caught with her pants down. I'd even say that I'd feel sorry for any idiot that comes calling on her."

She was in the limo with him when she noticed that they weren't going to the office. When she asked him about it he pulled out his phone and told the operator that he had something unexpected come up that she was to call him if she needed him. He leaned back in the seat.

"I want to spend the day with you going over the house. Then when we have all the measurements and a better list of what we might want, we'll come back into town and shop some more." He grinned. "Maybe we can go to that little shop that the last clerk was telling me about. They sell all sorts of women's apparel."

"What sort of women's apparel? And if you got a list of naughty stores from someone else, I'm going to hurt you." He flushed. "Damn it, Ryland. This is embarrassing. You have to learn to keep it in your pants."

She was suddenly across his lap. "I want you every waking moment. I'm hard most of the time I've not just finished making love to you and, even then, that's iffy. And the thought of stripping you down and seeing your lovely skin covered in silk and lace makes me dizzy."

"You're going to wear it out before we're old." She rocked on his hard cock and moaned. "Ryland, do you think the new mattress is there?"

He lifted her shirt and nipped at her hard nipple through her bra. She'd packed an extra pair of clothes today, but if he was going to rip them off her so soon she might be naked again before they made it home. She pulled her shirt up and over her head, then unhooked her bra and took it off.

"I have an extra shirt and pair of pants for you in my briefcase." He took her nipple into his mouth. "In the event that we couldn't make it until you were undressed."

The moment his hands curled into the top of her pants she moaned again. The sound of them tearing away from her made her wetter than she already was. She was over him now in just her panties, socks, and shoes. He pushed her back to his knees, unbuckled his belt, and then freed his cock.

She slid from his legs to the floor. He reached for her, but she took him into her mouth before he could pull her back up. He moaned loudly and held her to him. She licked him from groin to tip then back down again, taking in his tiny drop of cum at the eye of his cock

"Christ, you have a warm mouth." She pulled his pants down further as she took his head into her. Bobbing up and down, she took his pants down to his calves, making it so she could reach his balls. They were already tight and so heavy. Every time she pulled up, he would follow her by rocking upward. She was getting into a smooth rhythm of swallowing him down with every stroke when he tightened his grip in her hair and lifted her up.

"You keep that up and I'm coming down your throat. As much as I want to, I'd rather be inside of you when I come." She shook her head and took him again. "You'll pay for this."

He rocked up harder and faster. She reached between her legs and into her panties. She nipped at his cock when she touched her clit. He cried out and she looked up at him.

"Again. Do that again. But a little harder."

She bit him gently and was rewarded with a stream of precum. When she cupped his balls a little tightly, he nearly bucked her off him. Then he held her head tightly over him as she felt his first ejaculation hit the back of her throat. She pulled at his balls again and he cried out, his cock filling her mouth with his cum. Licking him clean, she sat back and let him see what she was doing. Her fingers were wet, and she was aching. "I love having you come down my throat."

He lifted her onto the seat and laid her back. She spread her legs and looked at him as he leaned down. She moaned when he moved her fingers and suckled on them. His fingers replaced her own.

"Come in my mouth." She nearly came up off the seat when he bit her clit. "Christ, do you have any idea how delicious you taste? Come now, Bronwyn, come hard."

She didn't mean to scream, she had tried hard not to, but when he pressed his finger past the tight muscles of her ass, she couldn't help it. As his tongue fucked her, his finger took her to new heights and she came apart twice more. When she lifted his head up, begging him to stop, he laughed.

"Any time you want to ride me in a limo, I'm all game. I will have to put up a better barrier between us and Charles, though. The poor man will be deaf if I don't." She looked at the glass between them and the driver. "He didn't hear you. I made sure of that. I was teasing you, love."

Ten minutes later they were pulling up in front of the house. She hopped out before the driver could open the door and she grinned at him. He smiled back and tipped his hat at her. Ryland told him that if he could come back and get them around dinnertime, he'd appreciate it. After Charles left, she and Ryland went into the house.

They had seen very little of it yesterday and now they explored. They went to the left out of the foyer and found a huge room. The chandelier was in the middle of the room and there was a nice fireplace against the wall. He told her a cleaning crew had come in and made sure that everything was put to rights. She looked out the large floor-to-ceiling windows on either side of the fireplace. Built-in bookcases lined the walls on either side of it and dark wainscoting lined the other wall. She loved this room immediately.

"I think this is the library. The specs said there was one and this would be the perfect room for it."

She nodded.

"The office is supposed to be next door."

In the office, his desk was sitting in the perfect place. She moved over to it and found the lamp already plugged in and a note on top of the desk. She turned to hand it to Ryland when she noticed he was still standing in the doorway. She asked him if he was alright.

"Did you see this desk before you got it for me?"

She shook her head.

"It's...Christ, Bronwyn, it's just like my dad's in his office. Exactly, including the lamp."

She looked it over and supposed he'd know better than her. She handed him the note from Alistair, who had come over to let the delivery person in. He leaned against the wall and handed it to her after he read it.

"Excellent choice. My God. How you found this thing is beyond me. If you ever want to get rid of it, let me know. I will pay whatever price you're asking for it. I can't believe you found it. Love to you both, Alistair"

She asked him what he meant.

"When Mom found the desk for Dad right after I turned five, the man who had it said that there were only two in the world like it. He told her that he'd made one for himself and one for his brother. But the brother had gone into a different line of work and hadn't wanted it. That was the one that Mom bought. Years later, after Dad passed away, we heard that the man had died as well and went to the auction of his home. The desk wasn't there. I've been looking since...so have Alistair and the rest of us. And you found it for us without even knowing it."

He ran his hand along the top of it and smiled at the small signature in the corner. She looked at it when he asked her to come and see it. She put her hand over it and felt the warmth and love of the man who had made it for himself, and his hope that his brother would love his as well and give up his notion of becoming an actor. She told Ryland what she'd discovered.

"I love you, Bronwyn. Not just for this, but because I simply love you." He held her for several minutes before letting her go slightly. "We'd better look around if we ever want to move in here."

She nodded. She'd never had a house before, and as they discovered each room and the small treasures left behind by the last owner, she knew that this one was special. By the time the limo came back for them, they had a huge list of furniture they needed, as well as a bigger list of things they needed to get in place. The house was perfect.

Kathi S. Barton

CHAPTER 13

They were just sitting down to dinner when someone knocked at the door. Sandra looked at her family and none of them seemed to know of any visitors. Bronwyn grabbed her hand and she stilled. Getting used to this girl was going to take some time, but she already loved her.

"He's here. Crawford is here." She looked at Ryland. "You have to stay here so that he doesn't know who you are yet. Let your mom go and I'll go—"

"You will not." Sandra had to laugh at the way Ryland thundered at her. "I will put this man in his place and he'll—"

"Kill you and your mom. We're not prepared for him." Bronwyn looked at her. "Tell him. Tell him that if he gets killed today that the man will stop at nothing to kill all of you. I'll be right behind the door. I swear he won't be able to harm you, but if Ryland pisses in his oats then I won't be able to help before some of us are killed."

"Ryland, let's do it her way. You can be ready in the event that he tries anything, but she's right. We have no recourse but to do it this way, to figure out what he wants."

Ryland sat down and looked around the room.

"She'll protect me. You know she will."

"I know it. I don't like it, but I know it." He looked at his brothers, who were as tense as he was. "Go to the doors and wait. Don't go outside, and shift if—"

"No. Don't shift until I say so. If they do, he'll know it. He'll take it as a sign of aggression, right?" Ryland nodded again at his mate. "I want you to trust me. I won't allow any of you to get hurt."

"It's not us he's worried about, sweetheart, but you." Sandra patted her hand and went to the door. When Bronwyn was behind it with her gun out Sandra saw her boys go to the other doors, each of them looking like they would rather be where they could watch her. She'd never felt so safe in her life. She opened the door.

"You sure took your time." He huffed at her and she nearly slammed the door back in his face. "I comed to find out if this here house has a male here. I want to talk to the male, not his lesser female."

"Do I strike you as a lesser female, young man?" He took a step back and she nearly followed him, but the hand at her elbow stopped her. "What do you want?"

"I done already told you. Where is your male? I know that he's here. There's cat everywhere." She watched as he raised his head to the air and sniffed. "Yep, cat."

"Well of course there's cat here. I'm a tiger, you idiot. How on earth do you expect there to not be a cat here? You knew that when you came here, did you not?"

He looked confused. She nearly laughed when the man standing next to him leaned in to whisper to him. "She's a cat, there'd be cat smells. Ask her about her sons. That's what we came here for."

"Where's your sons? Says here you got six of them." He looked at her suspiciously after consulting the paper twice. "Six sons. That's a lot of males."

"Yes it is. Six sons would be six males. You never answered my question. What do you want? And who are you anyway? I already answered the census questions years ago." He now looked so confused she almost felt sorry for him...almost. "Well? I'm waiting."

"You're supposed to be afraid of me."

She did laugh then. It was just too much. When he looked like he was going to come in the door, she pulled out the gun in her apron pocket. She'd been carrying it since she'd been living out here alone. He took a step back. "You come through this door and I will take your penis off at the root." She heard Bronwyn giggle and felt stronger for it. "I'm not one of those push-over types, and I know how to use this sucker. You get off my property right now or, so help me, you'll be losing an appendage you're fond of."

He looked at the man again, who said, "Your dick" before he turned back to her. "Now you listen here, I won't be putting up with you thinking that you can—"

The softly spoken *"shoot the deck"* through her mind had her firing so quickly that she nearly jumped herself. When he leaped back, she took a step forward and held the gun pointed at his groin. She'd had enough of this. "You come near this house again and they'll be wondering what sex you are when they find your dead body on the side of the road."

"You should know that I'm coming here as a mercenary." The man whispered again. "Emissary. I come here to talk to you about me razing your ambush. You shouldn't be treating me this way. Might go better for you if I was treated with a bit more respect."

"Respect is earned, not forced." She fired the gun again, this time over his head. "Get out of here before I lose my temper."

He left. Shifting on the deck and then lifting his leg on her flowerpot made her want to go out after him, but Bronwyn held her back again. She glared at the woman and nearly laughed on seeing her barely holding onto her own mirth. When she slammed the door, she turned to see her sons there, and not one of them looked pleased.

"You will not pee on my pot to re-mark it or, so help me, I will tan your hides. Literally." Sandra handed her gun to Bronwyn. "Would you be a dear and reload this for me, please? I have dinner on the table and it must be getting cold."

Bronwyn burst out laughing. When Sandra turned to look at her, she stood up and hugged her. It was the first time since she'd been there that Bronwyn had done it without someone hugging her first. Sandra held her tightly in her arms and fell in love with her. Good heavens, she had a daughter.

"You are the best. When you shot that deck, I nearly wet myself." With her gun in her hand, Bronwyn was still laughing as she went to the kitchen.

Sandra looked at her sons. "Well? You have nothing to say to me?" None of them moved. "I think I did very well for an old woman, if I do say so myself."

"Where...?" Ryland glanced at his brothers as he cleared his throat. "Where did you get that gun? And how long have you been carrying it?"

"You father gave it to me just after you were born. I was afraid most nights when he went off to work, so he showed me how to shoot it. He said he felt better knowing that I wasn't helpless. Smart man, your father. And I've been carrying it on my person since." She grinned at him. "I tuck it under my pillow at night too. So don't come in without knocking first. I may do you some serious harm."

All of them nodded and she had to bite her lips to keep from laughing. When she started to go toward the kitchen again she turned when Alistair called to her. She put her arms over her chest, thinking he was going to lecture her.

"Would you have really shot him in the groin? I mean, it was a great threat and one I would never have...one I didn't think you'd use, but a good one." She nodded and he laughed. "Bronwyn is right, Mom, you are the best."

As they entered the dining room Bronwyn handed her the gun and she put it back in her pocket. Dinner was a little chilled, but the atmosphere was a good deal more relaxed. When they all stood to help clear, Bronwyn stopped her.

"You know that we've just pissed in his oats, right?"

Sandra nodded and told her that she knew that she'd made an enemy.

"Well, you've actually made two. Cunningham will hear about this too and not be all that happy with the turn of events. I wanted to tell you something. Something that I'm sure you already know because of what you are. The gun is now loaded with silver. And when you shoot next time, go for the chest, as close to the heart as you can. Dead men can't shoot back."

It frightened her a little that Bronwyn wanted her to kill someone, then she thought of the man on the deck. He certainly wouldn't hesitate to kill her if he got the chance. She started to tell her that she would try and looked into the girl's eyes. There was fear there...for her she was certain. "I'll kill him. Any one that comes here, I will. I may be just a single woman with a gun, but I protect what is mine too."

Bronwyn nodded.

"I'm afraid."

"Good. If you're afraid, then you will be cautious. If you're cautious, then that's half the battle to winning." She hugged her again then picked up a stack of dishes. "Sandra, if you have to shoot someone to get to the bad guy, then do it. If you don't, all of us will die."

She didn't know if she could shoot one of her family to kill a bad guy, but she was very happy that Bronwyn thought she could. She took the last of the dishes into the kitchen to find that Bronwyn had put the men to work. Yes, she thought, she was going to love having a daughter in the house.

~~~

Eli fingered his gun as it lay on his desk. He looked at it rather than the man in front of him. If he had to see that stupid, moronic face once more before he calmed down he would kill him.

"I don't know why she tried to shoot me. And in my dick. Why on earth would that be the first thing that she wanted to shoot me at?"

Eli wanted to say that it was because she knew his brain was there, but didn't.

"And her house smelled like cats. Never smelled so much male in the house as she had."

"Six sons would do that." Eli looked up when the man behind him snickered. "You have something to add to this conversation, or are you just laughing at the fact that an elderly woman got the drop on you?"

"She said the same thing when he said that to her. He told her that her house was scented with males and she told him nearly the same words. That woman ain't like any of them other ones we razed. She's got balls." He snickered again. "Maybe more'n her sons do."

For some reason, he doubted that. She might have scared off Crawford, but she was still just a woman. A woman who shot the floor and made threats rather than simply taking care of the situation. He knew that she'd fall apart like most women did when it came to being brave. She'd get someone killed more than likely, and he liked that idea.

"I have an appointment with Ryland Golden on Friday to talk about him selling me Bronwyn. When he does, then I'll need to have the lab ready for her." Crawford raised his hand like a five-year-old. "Yes?"

"You said ready the lab up and we already got it all cleaned up with them humans. Or did you mean you want us to hire on some extra muscle to hold her still? Last time, she damned near killed a couple of my men. She's hell on us. You think maybe she might be madder at us when we bring her back?"

He actually picked up his gun. Shooting Crawford would make him feel better, but the other cats would tear him apart. There was no way for him to communicate with them and he didn't think he could control them with promises of money and whatever else they wanted. And what they wanted, he couldn't stomach. Killing. They stayed because they could kill however much they wanted and whoever they wanted to.

"Yes, she'll be madder. And for the record, not only will she be 'madder,' she'll be stronger. I noticed that when we went to pick her up. Her control has gotten much better."

"So she can do more stuff? Damn, but she ain't gonna like having us holding her down when you run them tests then, is she?"

Crawford looked at the man behind him.

"Remember what she did to him the last time she was there? Fucking bit him. Thought for sure she was going to take his hand off him."

Eli stood up. Both men looked at him and there was still a smile on Crawford's face. He wanted nothing more than to shoot him so that he'd have something else to remember, but he simply told them to get out.

"But you ain't never told us how we was supposed to—"

The gun was in his hand before he could think.

"You thinking of shooting me?"

"Seriously thinking about it. So if you want to live, I would suggest that you shut the fuck up and get the fuck out of here before I do. You've pissed me off enough for one day." Crawford started to speak again, but the man behind him clamped his hand over his mouth and practically carried him out the door.

Eli sat down. It was only Wednesday. Just two more days, three at the most, before he had her again, and then he was killing Crawford. Maybe even the rest of them too. Unless he could manage to get Golden to come work for him. The man was wealthy, of course—more so than anyone else Eli knew—but he was a smart man, a man who took risks, so Eli was going to try and talk him into being his partner. The money behind his brilliance, so to speak.

The phone ringing startled him. He rarely had anyone use his office line and didn't recognize the caller ID. He picked it up and said his name.

"So now you threaten older women, do you, to try and get what you want? Didn't really work out the way you wanted it to now, did it, Cunningham?" Bronwyn laughed. "Of course, you really didn't expect her to give me up, did you? I mean, come on, not everyone would sell out their own family like you did to get ahead."

"You mean the Golden woman? She was nothing. And when you come here again I'll show you how threatening I can be." Her laughter made him want to scream in frustration. "You'll not be laughing when I'm through with you, Bronwyn. And the harder you make me work at getting you, the more pissed I'm going to be. And you do remember what happens to you when I'm pissed."

"You remember what happens to me when I get that way too? By the way, how's the hand? Is it healing nicely?"

He looked down at the scar.

"Is the scar huge and ugly? Does it itch all the time so that you scratch it raw? You should watch that. It will get an infection that way."

He realized he was scratching at the scar and stopped himself. She laughed again. He was going to make her suffer for what she was doing. He found himself scratching his scar again and put his hand in his pocket. "I'll have you soon, Bronwyn. Very soon, and when I do, I'm going to make sure you can never bite anyone again." She tisked loudly at him. "You think this is a joke? You think that because you have a few cats at your disposal I won't be able to get you? Think again, bitch. When I find you, and I will, I'm going to tear you apart."

"You try that, Cunningham, you try. But know this." She was silent for several seconds before he started to see images in his head. Her tearing him apart. Then her cutting into him with long, sharp blades, knives he had used on her. He shivered when she rammed a sharp scalpel into his eye, and whimpered when she sliced open his chest. Fear crept along his skin until he was soaking wet in his own sweat.

She was sending him messages through the phone line. Eli slammed down the phone only to have it ring again. There was no way he was going to answer it, or the next two times it rang. He was suddenly afraid of her; terrified that she'd gotten so strong that she no longer needed to be in the same room with him to threaten him like this. Eli thought seriously about abandoning the whole thing with her and finding another way to fund his projects.

There was a message light on his phone and nearly erased it. But at the last minute, he decided to listen to it.

"This is Ryland Golden's office, and you had set up an appointment for this Friday. There has been a cancellation for tomorrow afternoon at three o'clock and, if you would like me to move your appointment to then, please call the office and ask for Monica. If there is no word from you by nine-thirty today, then I will call the next person on the list." She left a phone number and extension that he was to call.

It took him three times of writing down the number she'd given him before he got it right. The first time he forgot the extension number, and the next time he forgotten to get the name of the person he was to speak to. By the time he got through, she had to check twice to make sure she hadn't already filled it. He wanted to scream at her that she'd said she would give him until nine-thirty, and it was still only twenty-seven minutes after nine. He did have time yet.

"I'm sorry, sir, but I must check. I have you down for tomorrow at three. Please come at least twenty minutes early for your appointment so that you may be badged into the building. You will need to bring in a picture identification. You will also be wanded for any weapons, including knives, so please leave those in your car. Any delays in rectifying this rule will not give you enough time to get to the conference room. Mr. Golden will meet with you there." He heard her moving papers around. "Do you have any questions?"

He wanted to snap that he was just having a meeting, not going in to kill the fucker yet, but he only told her no, that he did not. Just as she disconnected he realized she'd said conference room and he wanted to ask her who all was going to be there, but didn't want to call back. It might piss her off enough for her to tell him that she had filled the appointment with someone else and he was shit out of luck.

He leaned back in his chair. The meeting would go well, he knew it. Golden hadn't gotten to where he was without doing a few illegal things on the side. He would bet that the man had his hand in all sorts of things that weren't as picture perfect as everyone thought.

Eli decided he'd look up more information on Golden. He wanted to be able to blow wind up his ass if that's what the man wanted. Eli had always been good at that, sucking up. He, too, hadn't gotten to where he was without a great deal of that. And a gun, of course. He wasn't all that thrilled about leaving his gun in his car, but didn't want to fuck up the opportunity to get Bronwyn back. He glanced at his hand.

It was bleeding. Eli hadn't realized that he'd been digging at it. Grabbing a few tissues off his desk, he wiped away the blood and looked at the scar. There was tears in his skin that ran deeply in two places, and had rubbed it nearly that deep in one more. He went to his bathroom to run cold water over it and decided he'd better get something for it before he did some serious damage. As much as he hated to do it, he called his doctor and told him he needed something for a rash. His story that he told him was he had touched seafood and now he was paying for it.

"I would rather see you, Mr. Cunningham, but I know you're a busy man. I'll just call something in. If it gets any worst, make an appointment and I'll have a look."

He told him he would, then sent his housekeeper to the drug store to get it. By the time she got back with it he was holding an ice pack over his hand and trying his best not to touch the now raw wound. He was going to fucking kill Bronwyn for this.

CHAPTER 14

"Just so you know, I'm not thrilled about this."

Bronwyn grinned at Ryland.

"You think he's stupid enough to think that this meeting is going anything but my way?"

"Yes. Yes, I do. He believes that anyone with half a brain, which is all he has by the way, will jump at this opportunity to make money. Even if you do have it all."

Alistair laughed, then coughed when Ryland glared at him.

"Oh, leave him alone. This was partly his idea too."

"Mine? I don't think so. All I suggested is that we get this meeting over with so we can figure out what he really wants." Alistair got up to go to the small refrigerator in his office. "There are things going on here that we know nothing about. Like this lab he has going. He has all the permits and paperwork in order. There is nothing wrong there that would make anyone suspicious about the real nature of what he's doing in there."

Bronwyn took the water he offered her, as did Ryland. There were still things she hadn't told them, like that she'd called him. Also, she hadn't told them everything she could do. She supposed it was time to say something, but she didn't want to. Bronwyn really liked this family and didn't want them to think any less of her. But when she saw Cunningham tomorrow she might have to do something to him, and she didn't want them to be freaked out.

"Just tell us." She looked at Ryland when he spoke. "Whatever you have going on, just tell us. We'll feel better, and then maybe the pencils on my desk will stop dancing."

"Sorry." They stopped moving. "That happens when I have pent up energy. Mostly I can burn it off by cleaning, but your mom is just too good. I have to tell you guys something. I don't want you to think…it's not horrible. Well, maybe it is if you want to think about it. I mean, not anyone else I know can—"

"Bronwyn. Just tell us. Whatever it is, we won't think any less of you. You're already scaring the shit out of Alistair."

She grinned at him.

"Now, tell us, if you please. I have a powerful need to toss Alistair out of my office and make love to you again."

Bronwyn flushed and Alistair laughed. Sitting down again, she looked at Ryland. She was in love with the man, she'd figured out last night. And now she was about to fuck it up by telling them what else she could do. Thinking it was best to get this over with, she looked at the picture on the wall behind him, not wanting to see the look on his face yet. "I can read anyone's mind. I don't even have to know them, but just concentrate on an image of them or even see them, and I can see their every thought and their every memory. It's not something I do often, but it has kept me alive a few times. But I can't read either of you." Alistair shifted on his chair and she glanced at him. "I told Ryland about it, and now I'm telling you."

"But you can communicate with us?" She nodded. "I'm sorry, I don't see the difference. Why not us?"

She shrugged. "Right now, your brother Brock is hitting on the woman in his office. Neal is trying to decide if he should buy another suit, quit his job, or keep at it. I think he needs a vacation from life for a while. Keith is buried deep in a project that I asked him to look into, and enjoying himself."

"And Jules? What is he doing right now?"

She laughed at Alistair's question.

"What's he doing, fucking his assistant?"

"As a matter of fact, he is. Right there on his desk. She's screaming out his name and telling him to go faster and—"

"Okay, enough. I get it. You can read them. But why not us? And why is that important that we know?"

She got up to pace and tried to think how to answer Alistair's question. "I can control them because I can read them. When you guys were helping me with Cunningham, I knew that Jules was going to try and step in front of the moving car to scare the man driving it away. I let him know that doing that would get him killed. Yesterday, when Crawford came to the house, I knew that Brock was about to shift to go to the aid of his mom when the shots were fired. He would have gotten hurt and hurt your mom in the process. I can't control you." She could tell that Ryland was pissed, but she wasn't sure why. Did he really expect her to step back and let them get hurt when she could keep that from happening? Not fucking likely. When he opened his mouth to speak, Alistair stood up and started pacing.

"You said that you can control people. And obviously cats too. Does that mean you can control all living things? Even in the wild?" She nodded. "Okay. Bear with me here for a minute. You were in the lab with Cunningham and he hurt you. A great deal. Why didn't you control him or the others to make them stop? Why was he able to get...? You can't control him either."

153

"I couldn't, no. But I can now." She took a deep breath before continuing. "I called him yesterday. Cunningham, I called him. Right before you did."

"You called him without telling me?" She nodded at Ryland. "Why? Did you think to, I don't know, make a deal with him? One to keep us safe because you think we can't help you?"

That hurt her, and she was pretty sure he knew it. Before he could say anything else, she picked up the file on his desk and handed him the picture of Cunningham that had come with the information about the lab. "He has a scar on his right hand. It's a bite mark, one I gave him. It's nasty in that when I did it, I tore at him and nearly had his thumb off. But he punched me in the head and I dropped to the floor. The next time I woke up, I was—"

"Finish. Tell us what he did to you after you bit him. I know you're telling us about the scar for a reason, but I want to know what the son of a bitch did to you in retaliation."

She didn't look at Ryland as she answered him. "He had me tied to the ceiling. My feet were about five inches from the floor, and I couldn't touch it even if I stretched my toes. The ropes had burned into my arms from the day before, so now there was blood running down my arms. My legs were tied to the floor this time so I couldn't grab anyone when they got too close. I was naked." She closed her eyes as she thought of the way she'd hurt. "He had hung me there often those first few weeks. My arms would ache for hours after he let me down. This time, he was going to beat me. The whip, braided leather, had been tipped with barbs, he told me, to get the optimum pain from its victims. The first time it hit my back I screamed. Then, after that, I didn't make a sound. He was so pissed that he couldn't hear me again that he—"

"That he hit you more. Hurt you more."

She nodded, but didn't turn to look at Alistair.

"Then when that didn't work, he did what?"

"He let Crawford beat me. But he used his fists and his belt. He nearly killed me." She turned to look at both men. "But things have changed. I can control him. And I have. His hand where I bit him? It's going to be bothering him. I would say by the time he gets here tomorrow he won't be able to use it. Not without a great deal of pain. He'll not be able to use his gun or his whip for some time, maybe forever, if I can continue to make him believe that it's infected and itchy."

"Remind me never to piss you off." Ryland laughed when she started to tell him she couldn't hurt him when he continued. "You have more to tell us, what is it? And why us? Why aren't we telling the family?"

Okay, here went the hard part. "Cunningham doesn't just want me for my ability to move things. He wants me because I can kill. I can kill a person who is miles...hell, hundreds of miles away. Destroy them in such a manner that no one would ever be able to pinpoint how it happened. But I can't kill him."

"Why? It seems to me that all this would be over if you would simply reach out and take the man's heart out. If he has one." Alistair looked at her, then Ryland. "Bronwyn, what else aren't you telling us?"

"She can't kill him because he is somehow responsible for why she can do this. Am I right?" She nodded at Ryland. "And he has...what? Programmed you somehow to not be able to kill him at all? That's why he is so bold, because he knows that you can't hurt him."

"I can hurt him. A great deal, but I can't let it get to the point where he may die from the injuries. I can do it all the way up until it becomes life threatening, then I have to stop."

"You might not be able to, but I sure as fuck can. You weaken him, love, and I'll finish him off." Ryland laughed. "This has suddenly gotten a whole hell of a lot more fun."

~~~

Ryland watched her move about the house. The furniture had been delivered that day and it looked great. But he could tell that something was bothering her, because he'd been talking to her for over ten minutes and she'd not said anything. He sat on the new sofa and watched her pick up the little candy dish again and set it back down.

"There are groceries here now. Would you like me to fix you something to eat?" Nothing. "I think there might be a yak in there. How about a yak steak and fries?"

"The security system here sucks."

He nodded.

"I think your mom could get past it without much trouble."

"I hired a firm to come in and set one up for us this weekend. They're the ones that take care of the Towers." She paced more. "Bronwyn, what is it, honey?"

"I don't think this is a good idea." He started to ask her what she meant when she continued. "I can get you hurt, and your family would be hurt without you. There are just too many factors that can go wrong with Cunningham and Crawford. He isn't going to like that you're going to turn him down."

He supposed he should be happy that she didn't think he'd give her up, but he was still pissed at her. She had no faith in him whatsoever. Trying to regain control of his temper, he watched her closely. She was limping. "What happened?" He stood to go to her and she backed away. "Either show me or I'll tackle you and find out on my own. I mean it, show me."

She lifted her pant leg and he saw the long gash in her calf. Swearing, he picked her up and took her to the kitchen where he knew there was a first aid kit. She told him it wasn't all that bad.

"We were fucking around and shouldn't have been, now that I think about it. I asked him to show me how he shifted and he said no. Then I thought about pissing him off, and that got me what I wanted. Sort of. I didn't necessarily want to be clawed." She jerked away when he wiped the long wound down with a rag. "That fucking hurt worse than the claw."

"Which one of them is about to be killed? I swear to Christ, I'm going to beat the living shit out of whoever did this to you." She laughed. "What the fuck is so funny? One of my brothers hurt my mate."

"No they didn't. Max did it." He looked at her, confused. "The man at the gate. He's a bear. And I don't know about you killing him. He has a wife and five kids to support. He used to be a performing bear for the circus until someone saw him shift. Then it was all over for that career. I think he said that his trainer knew, but I don't know how he couldn't. Not as good as he was at some of his…. Are you all right?"

"Max the Bear from the Three Ring?" She nodded. "And he's now guarding the gatehouse?"

"Yes, but I don't think he wants to be called Max the Bear. His children don't know anything about that." She took his hand. "That's why I should go before anyone else comes here and gets hurt."

He looked at her calf and tried his best to wrap his mind around what this had to do with Max and him shifting and her taking off. He looked up at her face and saw that she was serious about this. He held her leg and sat down on the kitchen chair.

"Okay. I want to start over." He leaned down and licked a path the entire length of the wound. "Why did you want Max to shift?"

"You can't do that." She nodded to her leg. "What if there was an infection or something? You can't just go around licking people's sores and not get hurt by it."

"My saliva will heal cuts like this one. See?" He showed her the healing wound. "I can't do anything about deep punctures, but I can heal this. Why did you want to see Max shift?"

"I've never been a bear. And that makes sense, I suppose, when you think about it. They say that an animal's mouth is cleaner that a human's. But it could be dangerous if you—" He put his hand over her mouth and she stopped talking.

"Bear. You're going to tell me what you meant by you've never been a bear. Are you able to shift?" She nodded, and he was glad he was seated. "What can you shift into, anything?"

She pulled his hand away. "No, not anything. I can't shift into something without a heartbeat or less than fifty percent of my body weight or mass. And it helps me if I can see the person shift. I usually don't have someone to watch like I did Max, but I can work around that."

She could shift. He had no idea why that made him both thrilled and pissed, but it did. He tried to think of anything but her beneath him as a cat, but couldn't seem to make his mind get past that. When he stood up, he started taking off his tie. "You're going to shift and we're going out in the back and play around. Then I'm going to fuck you." His shirt was next, along with his jacket. "You're not getting undressed. I need you now and I want to take you like a cat."

"I don't need to strip. I can shift with my clothes on and then, when I'm human again, I won't be naked. I've never had sex as one of my pets." He grabbed the back of the chair as he thought about what she was saying. "Ryland, you don't look so good."

He moved toward the door and shifted as soon as the door was open. His pants still clung to his leg and he tore them off him with his teeth. She came out onto the deck and watched him for several seconds.

He was ready to go to her when she put her hands on the rail around her and stretched. Her cat took her in small measures. He would never be able to describe this to anyone else, neither would he have believed it. Her cat moved along her body like it was dressing her in fur.

And holy Christ, she was beautiful.

I don't always get the fur right. I can see animals in the zoo, but they're different than the ones that are were. Seeing you like this and all the others, it helps me get a better cat when she comes out.

He nodded to her and laid down to wait for her to come to him.

I thought I should have been smaller, more like my size, but you're not when you shift, are you?

No. I have to be bigger as a cat so that I can dominate others. The male can weigh up to five hundred pounds of muscle and bone. Other males as a were can be larger too, but not as large as the male. He watched her leap from the deck. *Come here, Bronwyn. I want to run with you.*

Not yet. I want to show you something. Please don't say anything just yet about this. I want you to...I've wanted to show you for weeks. She shifted to human again and stood before him for several seconds, dressed as she had been before. Then she was cat again. Before he could tell her he believed her, she was bear, then wolf, and then she was human again.

You're amazing. She moved toward him slowly as a tiger and changed colors from gold to white as she did. *You can be anything of any color.*

Yes. White is actually what I normally am when I'm a cat. I like it better for some reason. I feel...I don't know, I guess I feel like it's the real me.

Ryland could understand that. He loved being a cat, but hadn't been out to play in months, maybe even years. He stood up when she got close enough to him and he nipped at her shoulder. When she took off running he watched her until she was out of sight before he thought to chase after her. He found her deep in the forest a few minutes later.

They ran through the woods for over an hour. Every time he was close enough to her to roll her to the earth floor, she'd take off again. He knew that he could hold her there if he really wanted to, but he was enjoying himself entirely too much at the moment. When they stopped by a small pond about four miles from the house they both sat near it and drank deeply.

I'm starving.

He grinned at her. He was too, he realized. She moved up next to him and rubbed along his flank. She purred deeply as she did it.

I would like to take you right now, but I think that we should go in and have some dinner, then I'll let you ravish me afterward. He laughed when she told him she'd have to think about it. *I love you. Let's go in before I forget my better intentions and take you anyway.*

They had a huge dinner and then made love on the floor in front of the fireplace. It was slow and easy, and both of them were exhausted after. He carried her up to their bed and crawled in beside her. Ryland held her to him as he drifted off to sleep. Tomorrow night he was going to take her in the yard and ravish her again, this time as his cat.

CHAPTER 15

Eli showed up at twenty after two. Making sure he had his driver's license as well as his passport with him just in case, he also checked his clothes three times to make sure he didn't have any weapons on him. He even took off the small ankle holster he had…not that he could have used it.

Glaring at his hand, he was pissed that he had to have it wrapped before he left the house, and his sheets had to be changed because of all the blood on them. Eli had scratched at his skin so badly through the night that he would have to have stitches if he kept it up. He could feel it burning now, the need to scratch it again.

Eli had woken up that morning with his hair brush in his hand, rubbing it against his already raw hand like it was a lamp and he was going to get a wish granted. And it fucking hurt. Glad now that he'd taken something for the pain, Eli knew if he hadn't he might not have been able to make this appointment. He was going to give his cook a bonus when he got home for having painkillers on him. Eli smiled again at the security officer.

"You're a mite early for this appointment, aren't you?" It was now twenty till three. "I mean, most people don't show up until the exact moment they have to, and are late because I have to check them out before they can go up."

It was on the tip of Eli's tongue to tell the man that he was a professional and not some idiot from the streets, but he only nodded. When he and Golden did business together, he was going to make it one of the stipulations that he fire this ass. The elevator ride was made in silence. Lieutenant Flores might have been saying something, but he was speaking so low that Eli had neither heard him nor really cared. When the doors opened, he nearly stepped back. There were more men there than had been in security when he'd come in.

"Mr. Cunningham, I'm Ryland Golden. These are my brothers Alistair, Neal, Brock, and Keith. Jules will meet us later. They're all partners in this firm with me. And this is my mother, Sandra Golden, retired."

He shook hands with each of them and eyed the matriarch of the family, trying to associate the woman who stood before him to the gun-toting grandmother Crawford had described.

"And this is my wife, Bronwyn Golden."

His hand suddenly started to burn. It got so bad that he dropped to his knees and held his wrist, knowing that it was going to be in flames at any moment. Glancing up at Bronwyn, he saw that she was laughing at him and he nearly lunged at her, but suddenly he was lying on his back with a boot on his chest.

"There are a great many things that I'll tolerate, but you touching my sister-in-law isn't one of them." The man Golden had called Brock leaned down to his face as he continued. "I would really enjoy ripping your fucking throat out for what you've done to her, but she said we have to play nice. At least until you piss her off again. Which I'm betting won't be long in coming."

He was helped up so quickly that he nearly fell over when his feet touched the floor again. He tried to speak through his anger, but he was too pissed to think. She was his wife. He had married the cunt, and now he would have all the say in what she would do.

Eli looked at Golden and smiled. "So, you're her husband. That's very nice. I'm sure she's told you a great many things about me, but has she told you what she is? What I've made her to be?"

"They know everything, you twiddle dick."

He took a step back and came up hard against another person. He was really between a rock and a bitch now.

"Ah, Jules. Come on then, let's get this meeting over with." Ryland led the way and Eli had no choice but to follow. He was flanked on all sides, and he watched as Bronwyn held hands with her husband. This was something he hadn't expected. Not even close.

They all sat around an oval conference table with Ryland at the head and him in the middle. Bronwyn sat across from him, and he noticed that Brock stood behind him. He felt like a speck on a microscope. He looked up when Ryland said his name.

"You had a deal to talk to me about? Something about doubling my worth?" The arrogant ass leaned back in his chair and Eli found himself wanting to snarl at him. "I'm worth just over five hundred billion; I'm not sure what I'd do with more than that. I have all I need right here in this room. Minus you, of course."

"Of course." He looked at Bronwyn. "She's worth a great deal more than that; are you aware of that? She can do things that would make you twice or three times that amount. All you have to do is make her cooperate with me and I'll share the wealth with you."

Ryland laughed, startling him out of his mental picture of what he'd do to the woman first. Eli looked at Ryland to see that he wasn't the only one laughing; they all were. And he was pretty sure he was the butt of their humor.

"You know her, right?"

Eli nodded at the man called Alistair.

"Then you must know that no one, including her husband, makes her do anything. She's a...my dear sister is an entity unto herself."

"But you should make her." He looked around the room to see that he was making no impact on these people at all. "She's worth millions just for the things I've given her. As her maker, she should just do as I tell her, but she's a stubborn bitch who thinks that—"

He was suddenly across the room, looking up at the ceiling. When a shadow made him look to his right, he cringed away from the biggest fucking tiger he'd ever seen. Then he heard Bronwyn speak.

"I wouldn't, if I were you. Run, I mean. Or maybe you should. That could be an adventure for you." She laughed. "Tigers like to play with their food, did you know that? And this one is very hungry."

"Is he going to kill me?"

She reached over and stroked the big cat's neck before looking back at him. He thought that, at that moment, he was more afraid of her than the cat.

"No. I won't let him kill you. Yet. I'm afraid you might make him ill." She leaned down and spoke to him. "But that doesn't mean any of the others might not kill you."

Eli looked at the others. Five more cats milled around the room, each of them snarling and swiping in his direction. Then it occurred to him. He looked back at Bronwyn. "The cats from the warehouse. You belong to them." She shook her head, then smiled. "You can't make me believe that they belong to you. You're nothing but a creation from my lab. A mistake made that thankfully hadn't been destroyed when you blew up the other lab. You owe me for even being alive."

The big cat put his paw on Eli's chest and pressed him back. The bite of his claws tore into his shirt, and he could feel the blood starting to run down his side. He looked over at Bronwyn, ready to beg her for his life.

"Ryland wants me to tell you something. He seems to be under the impression that you'll listen to him, when we both know that you're either too stupid or too arrogant to listen to good advice." She put her hand on the paw and pressed harder. "Are you listening to me, Cunningham?"

"Yes," he nearly screamed, the pain was so intense. "Tell me, damn it, so he'll let me the fuck go."

"He said that you're to leave me alone. And not to call or contact any of his family again." She grinned. "Alistair wants to know if you need him to have someone write this down for you? Anyway, you're to never call or...you get the picture. Stay the fuck away from his family. And just as an added bonus to your hurt little hand...."

The blade came out so quickly all he saw was a blur. When she stood up, blood poured from his cheek where she'd cut him. Putting his hand to his face to feel what she'd done, he could feel the bone and muscle exposed. His blood poured over his fingers and onto the carpet beneath him. He rolled to his knees; he was going to crawl from this place if he had to. These people were nuts.

"Let me help you."

Eli cringed from the guard that was standing just inside the door.

"You really shouldn't piss these people off. They tend to shoot first then ask questions later."

Standing in the elevator, he saw himself in the mirrored doors. He looked like he'd been in a horrific accident. Not only was he covered in blood, but his shirt was ripped to shreds and his hair was standing on end. He glanced at the guard behind him. "They'll pay for this." The man nodded and told him to try and send them the bill. "I don't mean my medical wellbeing, you idiot. I mean they'll pay for humiliating me and cutting me."

"Nah. I wouldn't count on that either if I was you. One thing I've learned over the years of working for the Goldens is that they don't cheat, nor do they retaliate. Could be they'll make an exception in your case, but maybe not." When Eli turned to look at the man, he smiled, and Eli nearly fell out of the elevator when it opened. The man was gone and in his place was a large wolf.

Eli ran to the doors only to be stopped by another guard. When he asked for the badge, Eli nearly threw it at him when the large wolf moved toward him. This place was a fucking mad house. He had the door open to his limo before the driver could get out all the way and he screamed at him to drive, just drive.

He was nearly to the hospital when he realized that he had something in his coat pocket. Taking it out with trembling hands, he laughed at the five hundred dollar bill and the note attached. "For medical expenses." He was still laughing when he was taken back to a room. Yes, he was going to kill them all. Especially that fucking cunt Bronwyn and her husband.

~~~

"That was fun."

Bronwyn looked at Sandra, who was helping her wipe up the blood from the carpet. Ryland and the others had gone to dress and, when she sat on the floor to start cleaning, Bronwyn joined her. It had been fun, but also dangerous.

"Did he really make you?" She looked up at Jules as he and Ryland walked into the room. "He said that he created you and that you owe him. Is that true?"

She nodded and continued with what she was doing. "In a way, I suppose. I was born in a regular hospital to a single mother. I guess I had some abilities, mind crap and a higher than average IQ. But I was semi-normal. Then I was tossed around for a while until I was with a streak of cats that were razed by Crawford."

"He found you there because of Crawford." She nodded at Ryland. "Why didn't anyone try to help you after your mom was killed? Didn't they care that you were being abused by him?"

"Probably not. I was sort of out of sight, out of mind by then. And much too old for anyone to want to adopt. And as I had no living relatives I was sort of shit out of luck. Then Cunningham found me; not really sure how, but then he took me in and made sure that I was…cared for, I suppose you could say." She looked at him. "Why did you tell him I was your wife?"

"Because you are in the eyes of my kind. And as soon as we can arrange it, I would very much like for you to be in the courts as well." He took her hand. "Did that upset you?"

"No. I was surprised is all. I wasn't really cared for so much as I was a guinea pig for whatever he wanted done."

He let her change the subject for now.

"He experimented on you?" Jules looked at Ryland when she nodded. "He can't be allowed to walk around after that. You are going to do something, aren't you?"

"I will."

His mom stood up and took the rags from Bronwyn as she left the room, taking Jules with her.

Bronwyn looked at the mess, then at Ryland as he stood in the doorway. "Say something." He continued into the room and closed the door behind him. She thought he was going to sit down, but he held out his hand to her and she let him lift her up. She was cuddling into his chest when she started talking. "He had them inject me with all sorts of formulas. Most of them were things I'm sure he had no idea what they'd do. But the things that enhanced me seemed to have double the effect. Then he started injecting me with serums. Things like wolf venom and other shifters. At first, he didn't think anything had worked. And I suppose it hadn't. Not until later."

"Not until puberty set in."

She nodded.

"It's the way of all weres. We're trained up until then to know what we're supposed to have happen, but it won't actually take effect in us until then."

"I'd already escaped the first time by then. But he caught me again later." She moved to one of the chairs and sat down. "He had had some results. I could move things with my mind before, smaller things, but by the time I'd been ready to leave I could move nearly anything. And I could control people. He didn't know about that, I'm not even sure he knows now, but I could and can. He just assumed because I wasn't showing him results that there were none."

"You hid them from him and everyone else. How did you escape? I'm sure now it wasn't a case of him letting you go when he thought you weren't living up to his expectations. How did you manage it?"

"I waited until there was hardly anyone in the building and unlocked the door to my cage. By the time I had made it through the building I'd gotten all the cleaning crew out, as well as any security. They weren't a part of what he was doing so I had no reason to hurt them. There were a few others there. Some like me that were there as projects, he called us, but others that he was using as specimens." She looked at him. "Two of them didn't want to leave and I couldn't make them."

"It's not your fault. They could have left." He sat down beside her. "We're going to get him, Bronwyn. I swear to you that we will. He and Crawford are going to pay. Pay with their lives, if I have anything to do with it. Men like them are not worth you getting upset over."

She grinned up at him. "You nearly had him piss his pants when you put your paw on him. Christ, I could smell the fear on him."

"And he left here like we were chasing him. I swear to you, since I've met you, I've never had so much fun. And I've gotten to know my tiger a great deal better as well." He lifted her from the chair. "Do you know what I'd like to do right now if I didn't have this meeting that I have to attend?"

She slid to the floor and ran her hands up his thighs. He watched her as she pushed him back a little and put her hands on his belt. He felt his cock lengthen and thicken at what she was going to do for him.

"You seem so tense. Do you think you'll make it until you come home if I helped you a little?" Her voice was like pure sex, and he shivered when she put her fingers on the clasp at his pants. "What do you want, Ryland? Me to suck on you until you come down my throat, or would you like to take me on the table behind you?"

He glanced at the table then back down at her. "Both. I want to feel your mouth wrapped around me again, then I want to pound into you until you come on that table. Do you think it'll hold us?"

She eyed the table as she reached into his pants. Hissing through his teeth, he lifted his ass up so she could pull them down further. Ryland nearly fell off the chair when she nipped hard at his cock. "Gently, love. If you do that again it'll be over before you start." She grinned seductively at him and he knew he was in trouble. "Bronwyn, no."

It was too late. She took his balls into her mouth and rolled them. Gripping the chair harder, he rolled his hips upward. When she took him into her mouth, he did cry out when she bit him. He was going to come right now if she kept it up, and he wasn't sure if that was a good thing or not. Her hand slid beneath him the next time he rocked into her warm mouth and he trembled with anticipation.

"Come for me, Ryland. I want to feel you come down my throat again." Her command had him grabbing her head and holding her over him as he fucked her. When her fingers slid over his puckered ass muscles, he tightened his grip, knowing that as soon as she entered him, he was gone.

He exploded. Not just his cock, but his entire body came. His eyes rolled to the back of his head and he felt the room dim. She never stopped, not with her mouth or her finger inside of him. He never knew that pain could be so amazingly wonderful.

Lifting her head from his cock, he begged her, pleaded with her to stop. He was hurting now it felt so good. She licked the last of his cum from the tip of his cock and watched him. He would be lucky if he could move in a month. He looked down at her through his hooded eyes. "I can't move."

She laughed.

"I'm serious. If the place caught on fire, I'd be fucked."

"Yes, you would." She stood up and sat on the chair next to him as he straightened his clothes. He wanted her, but didn't know if he could or not. But he could satisfy her in other ways.

When he reached for her, she shook her head. "I'm going to expect to be satisfied a great many times when you get home tonight." She stood up when he did. "As a cat, as a human…anyway and every way I want you."

"Your wish is my command. I will do anything you want so long as you come here again and help me with my tension, let's say…." He kissed her mouth long and hard, tasting him on her. "Daily."

She nodded and giggled. They had very little time now before the meeting, and he was excited to have her input about the men there wanting him to invest in their projects. She was going to be busy tonight, and asked for extra juice to be put in the room. *Christ,* Ryland thought, *I love this woman.*

CHAPTER 16

They had a plan. And as soon as he had that fucking bitch in his possession he was making her take this hex off his hand, and would make her pay for what she'd done to him. And Eli knew it was her. She'd tried to ruin him.

His hand was now in a soft cast. He'd woken up after the meeting with the Goldens with his hairbrush again. He didn't even remember going to get it from his bedroom, but he had, and now he was going to need surgery to repair the damage done to his hand. He glanced at the hospital bill and snarled. She was so fucking going to pay.

The doctor at the emergency room had taken one look at his hand and had sent for a consult with another doctor immediately. Eli thought he was bringing in another doctor for a second opinion, but he'd gone to get someone to evaluate his mental stability. He damn near came up off the bed when he'd started asking questions.

"Why do you care what my financial situation is?"

The man had looked up from his clipboard and frowned at Eli.

"I mean, I have an injured hand and I pay my bills. What's the problem?"

"That looks self-inflicted, Mr. Cunningham. We just want to make sure that when we let you go home, no more injuries occur."

Eli thought it was his "we let you go" that had alerted him that things weren't what he'd thought.

"You can understand our concern, correct?"

"Not really. I have a seafood allergy. You can and should ask my own physician if you don't believe me." He moved to the side of the bed to leave as he continued. "I came here for help with my hand. Whatever you're inferring with your little clipboard and pen there, you can go fuck yourself."

He was nearly to the door when his doctor came around the corner. He wanted to snarl at him for telling Eli to go to the emergency room, that he'd meet him there and then not be there to treat him. He would have too if there hadn't been a cop standing so close. He told his doctor what they had tried to do to him.

"I've taken care of it for you. Come now, let's have a look at this."

Four hours later, he was not in nearly as much pain as he had been, and the itching was not as intense. He looked down at the cast and thought about what he was going to have to do to get his hand looking like a hand again.

He'd gone to the bone in several places when he'd used the brush. And on the back of his hand, near his thumb, it was raw and torn so badly that the doctors had thought there might be muscle damage. He was going to hurt Bronwyn in ways she couldn't imagine. Then Crawford had shown up at the hospital to bring him home.

"I want her and that ambush she's with tonight. We know where they are, and I want you to go and distract the cats while I get her." Crawford had laughed. "You better have something poking you to make you laugh right now, or so help me, I'll kill you."

"They call it a 'streak.' What a pussy name for a bunch of cats." He glanced over at Eli. "You ever heard of such a thing?"

They were actually both the same, but Eli figured that Crawford liked the word ambush because of the way it sounded. He had opened his mouth to tell him this when he thought better of it. The explanations and the conversation they would have about it would drive him insane.

"You just leave that streak of theirs to us. We got it. I'm thinking that we'll take that old lady's house too. We could make it into our sort of playhouse." Eli glanced at him when he laughed again. "Maybe can make it our headquarters. Have meetings and shit in it. Wouldn't that piss 'em off?"

"I doubt it since you'll have to kill them all to take anything from them. And just so you know, Ryland Golden is a huge fucking male." Eli thought about Ryland's paw digging into his chest. "And he's far from your average tiger. This man has smarts."

"Shit, I'm not afraid of him. All it takes is a good swipe to the neck and *poof*, he's gone." He drove for a few more minutes before he turned to him again. "I still get to fuck her, don't I? Bronwyn? I get to fuck her, right?"

"If you're into necrophilia, then I'd say it's fine." He grinned when Crawford looked at him. "You'll have to clear it with her first. She might not be up for it."

"Yeah, yeah. I'll do that. You think I could be a good necrophilia?" Eli nodded. "I think so too. Got all the right parts to make myself set up as king of that...what did you call it again?"

"Necrophilia. And as soon as I have Bronwyn I'll make sure you have all the right parts to be king. It would be my pleasure." Eli had leaned back in the seat and smiled. He smiled again when he thought about Crawford asking for some extra money to set her up as his queen for a few weeks. Eli said he could have all the money he wanted.

And now they were only a few hours from making it all happen. It wouldn't matter if Golden or one of his brothers killed Crawford, or even if the old woman did; he was as good as dead anyway, as well as all his minions. It was all starting to fall into place and Eli had never been happier.

The phone rang and he reached for it before he thought to check who it was. As soon as he heard her nasal voice, he started to hang up. He hated his ex-wife.

"I've been trying to call you for over two weeks. Where the fuck is that extra money you promised me for the extra hour I had to wait for you to come and get them last time?" He closed his eyes, not wanting to deal with her right now. "You said because you weren't on time you'd pay me. Where the fuck is it? I have expenses."

"I just bet you do. And if you would have looked on the last check I sent you, I added your payment. I divided up how much I pay you per hour a month and added that amount. I think I was more than generous. I was actually only forty-three minutes late, and I paid you for a whole hour."

It had come to six dollars and twenty-five cents. He'd never had so much fun writing out a check for her in his life. When she started screaming at him about calling the courts, he let her. He'd been doing some checking himself, and she actually made a great deal more money than he did at the moment. He should be getting paid, not the other way around.

"I'm going to fucking sue you. Do you know how much money I make an hour at my job that you made me late for?" He told her that she didn't work that night. "You're checking up on me?"

"Of course I am. You don't expect me to pay you forty-five hundred dollars a month without making sure that my children are well cared for, do you? I know every move you make, every dime you spend, and what you spend it on." The silence on her end of the conversation made him bolder. "Who's the fuck buddy this week? Is it still the guy across the street? What do you think his little woman would think if she knew he was spending his vacation fucking you on the couch I bought?"

"You mother fucking son of a bitch. You have no rights to spy on me. I'm stuck with your fucking kids all day every day while you get to do whatever the fuck you want. What if I told you that I didn't want them anymore? Huh? How would that be if I suddenly said fuck it and dropped them off at your doorstep?"

"Do it."

She sputtered several times before she said, "Fuck off."

"Thanks, but I've been there with you and I'm telling you now, it wasn't all that good and I had to fake it." He hung up, then set the phone so it would go straight to voicemail if she called him again. He was sick of her shit and hoped she dropped the kids off. He would love to have them back in the house full time. Plus, he wouldn't have to pay her any more, and that was a bonus in itself.

Crawford came in ten minutes later. He was dressed in tear-away pants and a sleeveless t-shirt. He sat—more like flopped—into the chair across from Eli, looking excited. When his leg started shaking, Eli looked at him. "Are you fucking stoned?"

Crawford nodded with a sloppy grin.

"You fool. Didn't I tell you that things have to go perfectly tonight? Do you think you're on your best game when you're flying like this?"

"I'm always on my best game. Damn, I was born the best. You just leave it to us, we're going to fucking smoke them cock suckers." He leaned back. "We are so ready for this it'll be like a walk in the market."

Eli hoped so. If Crawford didn't kill the cats, then they'd be coming for Bronwyn and she was a female, not a lesser one like Eli was used to seeing. Now she commanded respect from all cats, including the one in front of him.

They drove to the house and Eli looked around for the others. They were supposed to be at the meeting place in five minutes and there wasn't a single one of them around. He asked Crawford.

"I told them to be here." He frowned. "I think. Been so worked up....Yeah, I told them. Mikey says that they are running a bit behind on account of they needed to gas up. You suppose he was talking about the truck or them? I ain't riding with some of them if they stopped for chili again. Christ, they can smell a place up."

Eli walked away. When Crawford called his name, Eli continued walking. He had to be on the other side of the gates when they started the attack, and if he was a few minutes early, then that would be great. He could keep away from Crawford and chill out before he went after her. He reached into his pocket and touched the dart gun.

He was going to drug her, then drag her to his car on the other side of the compound. Crawford thought Eli was coming to help after the cats were all dead, but he was planning on Crawford and his ambush being killed. If he survived? Then there was another gun, this one loaded with a full clip that had Crawford's name on it. Eli was prepared too.

By the time he got to where he'd parked the car, he was hurting again. Eli wanted to take another painkiller, but was afraid of what it would do to his judgment. Knowing he had to shoot left-handed and that he wasn't all that proficient at it made him nervous. He stretched his neck muscles again and heard them pop in the waning evening. Looking out over the grounds he saw them; Crawford's cats were on the move. Eli leaned back against the car and waited. There wasn't any hurry. Everything at the lab was set up as well.

He'd had one of the doctors, one he could trust, get the cell ready for Bronwyn. He had told him what he'd wanted, and was sure that it was done. Eli wanted nothing to interfere with his work this time. The cell was perfect.

The walls were poured concrete. They had held her before, but there had been a window, as well as a door with a window. He'd had both of them replaced. The window was gone, and the door had bars and no glass. She would be able to be seen at all times, and there would be no danger of her waiting for them to come inside before they knew what she was up to.

She'd killed three men before when he'd had them tell her to stand back so they could enter to get her. That had only worked one time, then she would simply wait until they were inside before she attacked. He'd taken care of that too. The cell was small, much smaller than before. She'd be lucky if she could sit, much less stand in this one.

~~~

"They're on the south side now. A dozen about a mile from here, and two more a few feet back. The others on the north are coming in low. All of them have shifted." She opened her eyes and looked at all of them. "And they're higher than kites."

"Good. It'll slow them down. Where is Cunningham? Has he made an appearance yet?" Ryland stood near the crude map they'd drawn to keep track of everyone. "He's probably waiting for them to attack before he comes."

181

Bronwyn shook her head and pointed to the west side. "He's here. I think he's high as well, but…nope, pain killers. And they're wearing off. I can play with him a little if you want."

He grinned at her. "Behave. We do this fair so no one says we had an unfair advantage over them when we kill them."

"Spoil sport." She watched the others mill about the room talking and joking. They were nervous and she knew it. She thought about how to distract them and smiled.

"Did you guys know that I can tell when you're having sex?"

Sandra laughed, but turned it into a cough when they looked her way.

"Yeah. And I'm telling you guys right now, you suck at your techniques."

"Suck? No way. You're sleeping with the oldest man in this room and you think we suck?" Keith laughed as he moved toward her. "Maybe if you had someone younger, with a great deal more stamina, then you'd see it differently."

She snorted. "More stamina might just kill me. Besides, Ryland knows more about wooing a woman than any of you will ever be able to learn. He's got moves." She danced around the room. "That would kill a woman less than me."

They all laughed and continued the joking. Even Ryland got into it with her and the others. Sandra and Sindy simply laughed at them. When she went to get Sindy to dance with her, someone put on some music. For twenty minutes they forgot what they were doing and simply had fun.

"Stop." She stilled when she felt a movement from outside. "They're moving. Remember what I said to each of you. Listen to me. I won't let you get hurt, and if you can't hear me—"

"It means the fucking bastard has you and we're to come running." Alistair cuffed her gently on the cheek when she started to tell him that wasn't the plan. "We won't let anything happen to you either, Bronwyn. We need you too much not to save your ass too."

They moved out of the house and into the darkness. She stood in the living room and felt the moment that each of them were where they needed to be. She looked at Sandra and Sindy, who were going to be ready with first aid should anyone need them.

Sindy put her arms around her. "You're going to beat him."

Bronwyn nodded.

"If you don't then I'm going to come out there and kick your ass."

"You and what army?" She pulled back and looked at her friend. "Don't leave this house, either of you, no matter what happens beyond these walls. Unless you hear from me or Ryland, you stay in here. He won't be able to come in here, I swear it."

They nodded and Sandra hugged her as well. "You will come back here, right? You get hurt, I've got two gallons of juice that I squeezed for you this morning. I'm counting on you to see this through. Ryland needs you."

"And I need him." She looked around the house. "This is the first home I've ever been in. The first time in all my life that I had a mother that cared about me." Bronwyn left out the back door, slipping into the darkness as she felt Cunningham leave his car and make his way to the house. She was going to intercept him and make sure that when this ended, there would be no more problems with him or his lab. Ryland touched her mind before she shifted.

We never did get to play together as cats. I'm looking forward to it. As soon as this is over, we'll go on a long honeymoon somewhere deep in the mountains and come back when it snows. How does that sound?

She brushed at the tears. *Sounds wonderful. Do you think we could stay until the following snow? I love to run in it as my tiger. I think that's why I like the white one so much.*

He was quiet, and she knew that he was trying to say whatever it was he needed to tell her. She shifted into a sleek black panther and moved along the shadows, thankful for the cloudy night.

You don't think you're coming back, do you?

She stilled, wondering how he had guessed.

I got news for you, mate, you'd fucking better. I have plans to have you large with our baby this time next year, or I'm going to kick some serious ass.

Lifting her head to the air, she sniffed. He was close...Cunningham was very close. She dropped to the ground and waited until he walked past, her thinking about Ryland. *I would like that too, but you know as well as I do that we're working against great odds here. I can keep you all safe, but Cunningham is unpredictable. The cats aren't. Kill is the only thing going through their minds at the moment.*

You come back to me, love. I can't live without you.

She nodded as Cunningham stumbled by her.

Bronwyn, did you hear me?

Brock just killed the first cat. It's begun. Go to them and, if I can, I'll be there when this is over.

CHAPTER 17

Ryland was afraid. Not of the cats that now moved along the property, but for his mate. She would save them all and not herself if it came to that. He smiled when he thought of her dancing with Sindy and the others, and the look on his brothers' faces when she told them they sucked. She was going to be a great leader of these men, and he intended to make sure that she was there to do it. He waited while Cunningham moved past him before he moved.

What the fuck are you doing? He nearly leaped out of his skin when she whispered through his mind. *Get back to where you said you'd be. You and your brother are supposed to be watching the north area.*

I'm not leaving you. You can bitch all you want, but...are you a panther? She growled low through their link, and he grinned. *That is why I didn't see you at first. A fucking panther? Next thing you'll do is shift into a fucking dog or something.*

You get back there right now. I have this. She moved past him and he followed her. When she stopped, so did he. She turned to look at him, and he sat down.

I called in some extra help. Max said that he would help, as will his four brothers and his sister. They think this is a hoot. Stan from the building is at the house with his pack. They are looking forward to kicking some pussy; his words not mine. Oh, and Sindy said she wasn't staying out of this for all the money in the world. She is a beautiful cat, by the way.

She moved toward him and he stilled, waiting for her to swipe at him, but she only rubbed up against him.

You're going to be home tonight if I have to kick your ass to make it happen.

She turned abruptly and moved quickly toward the house. He wanted to ask her what happened, but she was moving so fast that he had a hard time keeping track of her. As it was, every time he lost her in the darkness he had to wait for the clouds to disperse over the moon to see her shiny coat. Finally, he saw where she was headed.

The man stood still as he took aim. Ryland tried to see who he was aiming at, as he didn't sense any of the other animals or his family nearby. But then he saw the cat stalking toward Cunningham. He moved up behind Bronwyn and lay very still.

"You can't possibly think that I'd let you be a partner with me after all this?" The large cat snarled at Cunningham. "You know, I think I can understand you better now than when you were actually speaking to me. Amazing. You're by far the stupidest man I know."

He's planning to blame you for his murder. He has been planning this for a very long time. Crawford is pissed, but more than anything, he's confused. He thought that they had become friends.

Ryland nodded.

This is going to end badly.

She shifted before he understood what she was planning. She told him to stay there in the event she needed him, and moved to stand in front of the cat. She reached out her hand, scratched him behind the ear, and everyone went still.

"He's thinking you might be kidding him. Crawford wants to know why you're doing this." Bronwyn looked at the tiger behind her, then at Cunningham. "He wants you to put down the gun before this gets dirty."

"It's ugly, you moron. Before it gets ugly. You stupid motherfucker, you could fuck up an escape out of a bag with a torch to help you."

Ryland moved forward slowly, an inch at a time.

"What the fuck are you doing, Bronwyn? Get out of the way so I can kill him and get you back to the lab."

Ryland was ready to attack when he noticed that two cats, not his family, were moving toward Cunningham. He took several steps back and lay down. When another set of them moved in from the rear, Ryland realized something else. The fighting had stopped.

"You should really have taken the time to get to know the people who work for you. I was just telling Ryland that the other day. You can't be too busy to make sure you're aware of everyone. They might come in handy someday." She grinned. "Did you know that there is a bear family that lives near here, and that—?"

"I don't give a good damned fuck who lives around here. I've had enough of your shit. Get the fuck away from him and over here where you belong."

Ryland nearly snarled, but caught himself. He looked at the movement from his right and saw the big black bear making his way slowly toward his position.

He's going to stand with you. Don't let Max get hurt, Bronwyn said to him.

Ryland looked at the bear as he came toward him. He had to weigh at least a thousand pounds. Who was going to protect him from the bear?

The other gun appeared in Cunningham's hand, and Ryland could smell the drugs. He was going to dart her. But before he could move to her one of the cats swiped at Cunningham's leg. The shot went way off its mark as he fell. The second shot, one that came from the regular gun, fired, but he was going after Cunningham and didn't see where it hit.

You hurt? She told him no. *Get to Neal. He's hurt and needs to get to the house so that he can shift safely and heal.* She told him she'd take care of it.

Don't kill him. He nearly tumbled over a log he was in the process of jumping over when she said that. *He has some information I want and if you kill him, I won't get it.*

He saw Cunningham then, running as quickly as he could, falling every few feet. He leapt at him the last five feet and took him down. Another cat, this one smaller than even Bronwyn's cat, stood nearby.

Cunningham was begging. He was promising him everything under the sun, things that would be impossible for anyone to think he would ever get from him. The most outlandish thing was a ticket on the next space shuttle to the moon. Cunningham apparently knew people.

When Crawford sat beside him, Bronwyn was with him. The cat was bleeding from the chest. He looked at her and she shook her head. The shot had apparently found a mark in the cat. He moved out of the cat's way when he put his paw over Cunningham's chest.

"He's giving you and me his ambush for this. He said we're welcome to them." He looked at the four cats near them and nodded to each of them. "Crawford said that there are others that he has at the lab too, humans mostly, that he wants us to care for."

Done. What does he want in return? She nodded to Cunningham. *He wants to kill him?*

"No. He wants them to." She nodded to his right and then pointed to his left. There were about two dozen tigers there, and most of them looked bloodied. He nearly asked her where the rest were when she spoke again.

"Your brothers are very good men. Will they be able to live with what they've done tonight?" So they had killed. "It was them or those dead tigers. They left them no choice."

They'll be fine. They'll feel like they've done right by their family, so they'll be more than fine.

She nodded.

What's he doing?

"You don't want to know." She moved past them and toward the house. "I have to do one more thing. Can you stay with your family until I get back?"

No. Let me come with you. She stopped and turned to look at him. *Please?*

"It's not going to be pretty. It's going to be…I've been in one of these labs before, you haven't. You'll be better off if you stay out."

He nodded, but moved with her when she started walking again.

"You're a stubborn ass, has anyone ever told you that before?"

Yes, as a matter of fact, they have. Alistair did. He said you and I were a perfect match in that department.

He followed her, stopping once to shift and change, and caught up with her in the driveway. She said that everyone inside was safe. He looked up at his mom when she waved at him. She looked worried too.

He got into the passenger seat beside her and she asked him once more if he wanted to stay behind. He put on his seatbelt as an answer. She shifted the car into drive and left the house. He tried to think what could be so bad at the labs that she was this sad about. Christ, he hoped this wasn't a mistake.

~~~

Alistair stared at the dead man, or what was left of the dead man. They had torn him apart. As soon as Ryland had turned his back and walked away with Bronwyn, the big cat with his paw on Cunningham's chest had roared. The other tigers with him had done the same. As soon as Crawford fell on top of Cunningham, he had scrambled out from under him—no small feat considering how big Crawford was—and ran. Big mistake.

Alistair and his brothers made their way back to the house as he thought of what the other tigers had done next. They had toyed with him, played with him, clawing at his flesh just enough to make him bleed, but not enough to kill him. When he drew his gun, one of the tigers lunged for it and was killed. Another tore Cunningham's hand off from the elbow down. His screams sent the other cats into a killing frenzy.

They pounced on him in seconds. Screams were long and loud as they tore at him. Alistair wanted to look away, but found that he couldn't, needing to make sure that the fucking bastard was dead. But he knew it was more than that; it was the fact that he simply couldn't look away from the carnage. When he heard bones being crushed in powerful jaws, he stood up slowly; when the screams suddenly stopped, he stood stock still, as did the rest of the family.

The larger cat stood near the dead body and roared again. As soon as the others joined in he stopped and looked at him.

Alistair knew that if he made any sort of sudden move he would be dead, so he only nodded at him. Then as Alistair watched, the big cat pissed on Cunningham's body. The rest of them did the same. He moved away, leading his brothers home when they finished.

Why did they do that?

Startled out of his memories, Alistair looked at Brock. *They all pissed on him...why? Were they marking him?*

I suppose you could call it that, but not in the way a dog marks a tree. They were warning others what could happen if they fuck with them. And their scent will make sure they know who killed him.

Alistair moved to the place where their clothes were and noticed that Ryland's were gone. He was relieved. He hadn't seen him in a while and was worried something had happened.

Finding his mom and Sindy in the house, he asked where Ryland was, and neither of them answered him. He tried contacting him, but he was either blocking him or Bronwyn was. He followed his mom into the kitchen when she said she was making sandwiches.

"She got into the truck and he went with her. I think they're going to that lab now." She sounded upset and he asked her what had happened. "Sindy told me some of the things that happened to Bronwyn at that place. She said that Bronwyn had nightmares still about it because of the things she'd had happen there."

She was crying when he took her into his arms. He wasn't sure what to tell her, and decided to say nothing. What could he say? That it would be all right? He had no idea. When she pulled away, she started to fuss with the luncheon meats, slapping it onto buns. When he took her hands, she looked up at him.

"What if she still wants to leave? What if she won't stay even after we all fell in love with her? And poor Ryland? He'll be beside himself if she leaves after this."

"She's not leaving." She shook her head. "No, listen to me, she's not leaving. She and Ryland are fixing up the big house he bought. She's putting down roots and is happy here."

"Will that be enough?" His mom put three more sandwiches together before she threw everything down on the tray and sat on the chair. "I have a good mind to give her a piece of my mind."

Alistair pulled out his cell and handed it to her. "I don't know if she carries one, but Ryland has one. Call him and ask to speak to her. Tell her what you think."

She snatched the phone from him and opened it. He started making the sandwiches more suitably then started to assemble more as he listened in on the conversation.

"I would like to speak to your mate, please." Alistair grinned when his mother snorted. "You put her on right now, and tell her I said if she doesn't want to talk and drive to pull over. I have something to say to her and it won't wait."

He wanted to ask her what was taking so long, but he could see his mom swinging her foot a mile a minute. It was a good indicator that she was pissed off. He put a large bowl on the table and filled it with the three bags of chips and other snack food he found in the cabinet. He was nearly ready to call in the others when his mom spoke again.

"You tell me right this minute what you think you're doing. And I want an answer as to why you didn't come into this house and tell me that my sons were all right. Don't you think I might have been just a little worried?" There was a long pause. "Well, that's not the same thing as telling me in person now, is it? I would love to have seen that you were all right as well. Made sure that you—"

He watched her shoot up off the chair as if she'd been in a cannon. He waited as she glared at the cabinets in front of her, and thought maybe this was not such a good idea. Then she started speaking again.

"When I ask you a question or am speaking, you do not interrupt me. I may be retired, but I'm still the head of this household, especially if you plan on abandoning us at the first sign of trouble.... You most certainly did so."

He handed the tray of sandwiches to Keith when he came through the door, and stood there waiting with the two bowls of chips in his hands to shove at the next person who poked their head in. It just happened to be Neal and Brock. He nearly knocked Jules over with a case of bottled water when he came through. Dinner was served.

His mom put the phone down and smiled. He wasn't sure if he should trust that or assume everything was fine. When she got up and started pulling out pickles and other condiments, he called for them to come back into the kitchen and fix their sandwiches. Each of them stared at her when she started humming. He realized they'd heard everything, including the phone conversation.

"Mom? What happened? Is she coming back with Ryland?" She nodded. "Is she staying?"

"Well of course she is. Why wouldn't she? I don't know why you were so worked up about it. Everything is just fine."

Alistair looked around, more confused than ever as she continued.

"There are times, Alistair, that I just don't know where your head is. Worrying over nothing like that. What are you going to do when you find your own mate?"

"I don't...I guess I just don't know." He sat down and picked up a sandwich. He was trying to wrap his head around the bizarreness of what happened when he heard Ryland.

There is no cell phone service here. Could you call for help? We're fine, but there are...Christ, Alistair, it's worse than...I was going to say worse than I thought, but I could never have imagined anything at all like this. They were cutting them up while they were still living.

He pulled out his phone, handed it to his mom, and mouthed for her to call 911 for the lab. She asked if they were all right and he nodded. She dialed and asked him the address. Ryland told him and he repeated it to his mom.

We're coming there now. Don't even try to stop us. Ryland said he wouldn't, but not to bring Mom. *I don't think you're going to be able to stop her. She's gathering supplies up now and having everyone put them in the trucks.*

Figures. He laughed slightly. *Did you know that Mom called Bronwyn? They got into it big time just before we got here. I think it was perfect timing. Is Mom okay?*

Yes. She blamed it on me. Is Bronwyn okay? The silence was telling. *I'm guessing not.*

No. She's moving through the building like she's on a search and rescue mission. That's pretty much what it is, I suppose. Ryland didn't say anything more for a long while until they were about half a mile from the building. *The code to get in is four-two-eleven. Make sure you close the door when you come in. There are still...things here that could get out.*

CHAPTER 18

It took them over a week to sort through the mess in the lab. Bronwyn moved through the building several times a day, looking for and helping to pull out bodies. It had gotten to the point at the lab that there had been too many to bury daily, so they'd started putting them in empty offices and stairwells. They found over two hundred bodies, and more than three dozen body parts that didn't seem to come from any of the dead. The people she was helping were appalled and in shock.

"There's a woman outside that says her husband owns this building and she wants to talk to him. Right now, she said."

Bronwyn looked at Mike Hopper as he delivered the message.

"She has two kids with her, and I think they belong to Cunningham."

She nodded and went to speak to the woman. Mike stayed at her side; the only time he left her was when Ryland was with her or she was at home. He hadn't left her since the night of the attack. He told her after what she'd done for his friend he could do no less than to protect her from now on.

"Mrs. Cunningham, my name is—"

The woman cut her off with a slap to the face. Bronwyn nearly didn't catch Mike before he attacked her. She saw Ryland coming toward her.

"You never call me that name again. And where the hell is my husband? That son of a bitch is taking his kids right now. I've had it up to my ass in problems with them, and if he thinks I'm giving up my vacation at the spa for some tramp, you tell him it won't work."

"I'm assuming you think I'm the tramp?" Bronwyn laughed and shook her head at Ryland when he stood beside her. "Mrs. Cunningham here is a tad pissy because her husband isn't here to meet and greet her."

The woman in question lunged again and Mike caught her. Ryland laughed. This was the most fun he'd had in weeks. Bronwyn looked at him and he shrugged. "You can tell her. The police pretty much put you in charge anyway. Tell her where her husband can be found." Ryland nodded to Mike and walked away.

"See that field over there?" Bronwyn pointed to where Cunningham's body still lay, way beyond where they stood. "He's just there, about three miles straight ahead of you. But you'll have to walk if you want to see him. The terrain is a mite off for a car."

Mrs. Cunningham glared at her. "Call him here. I'm not going to ruin my shoes to go out there and talk to him. Just tell him to get his ass over here and get his brats. I have a plane to catch."

"I can't call him. Well, I suppose I could, but he won't answer me. He won't answer you either." The woman huffed. "And being pissy with me isn't going to get you anything either. I've had a shitty week cleaning up after your husband, and I'm not in the mood to fuck with you."

"Why, you miserable piece of trash." This time when her hand came toward her, Bronwyn caught it. She slowly bent it back until the woman was nearly bent in half trying to keep Bronwyn from breaking her arm.

"Now we're going to do this a different way. One where you politely ask me a question and I answer it, maybe as politely. A sort of give and take thing. Now, you want your husband here, correct?" Her hissed yes wasn't great, but it was an improvement over her slapping Bronwyn. "Well, that's not going to happen. I don't have the manpower to pick all of his pieces up, and I'm sure after a week of lying out in the heat you more than likely don't want to see him anyway. He's dead, in case you didn't get that."

Mrs. Cunningham paled, but it didn't stop her from making more demands. "You'll tell me the truth or so help me I'll…I'll—"

"Yeah. You should have a threat right on the tip of your tongue. I find that practice makes perfect if you don't want to be floundering for one at a sticky time. Like me, for instance. I have two. My standard is 'tell me the truth or I'll shoot your foot.' I use that one when I'm serious, but not terribly so. Doesn't mean I won't shoot your foot; just means I'll reconsider if you continue to piss me off rather than make some redeeming comment. The other is—"

"Shut the fuck up."

Bronwyn nodded and winked at Mike. She took the woman down a few more inches until she was nearly standing on her head. "Good one, but not a smart one when someone is ready and willing to tear your fucking arm out from the socket if you continue to piss her off." Bronwyn got very close to her face and looked at her. "I'm not one to fuck with again, Mrs. Cunningham. I'm not in the mood, and I can tear your throat out before you can take your next breath."

She let her cat take her. Bronwyn dropped to her paws just as Mike grabbed for Mrs. Cunningham to steady her. She snarled at the woman, who simply fainted.

Laughing, Mike looked at her. "You're sure one to piss off, aren't you?" He lifted the limp woman up and carried her over to the tree. When he came back, he asked what he was supposed to do with the kids.

"Sell them?" She told him she was kidding. "Ask Sandra if she can help out with…why are you shaking your head no?"

"You know I won't leave you unattended, not without one of the others around."

She looked at him and tried to read his mind. It wasn't working with him either. She started to turn away when he touched her arm.

"You don't know, do you? You have no idea why we won't leave your side." She shook her head at him. "Cunningham was going to kill Forest, had been thinking about it for weeks. All of us had seen it…even Forest did sometimes. But he wouldn't believe it. He kept saying that it was just stress or some shit. But we all saw it. So why did you not let him?"

"I didn't stop him from killing Forest. You saw that Cunningham shot him."

Mike shook his head.

"I didn't save him. I wouldn't have after what he did to Sindy and the others."

"No, you wouldn't have. But you didn't have to let him kill Cunningham either." She started to speak, but he stopped her. "You let him be killed by the people he treated the worst."

She looked at the lab when Mike did. He looked like she had when she'd first come out. Used up and pissed, more savage than human. She realized then that he'd been a part of it too.

"You're a survivor like me, all of you are. What can you do?" He looked at her and smiled. "You're older, so either you were a donor or you were a recipient. I don't think he would have kept you around if you were a donor, so you had to be like me."

"Not as much as you, but a little. I can shift, but only to the cat, and I can't read minds. I can block you, but if you worked at it hard enough you'd break through. Some of the others have talents, but aren't very good with them. They need practice. As you said, practice makes perfect." She waited for him to continue and felt a frisson of fear settle over her. "You let me and a few of the others out the day that you blew the building. Told me the place could only win if I let it, and told me to get my fucking ass out before you threw me out."

"So you won't leave my side because of some sense of duty? I don't want you to waste your life for something as stupid as me kicking your ass when it needed it." He shook his head again. "Then what? Why do you hang around me like I'm worthy or something?"

"We watch you because Cunningham isn't the only one wanting you for a lab." He walked to the car, but never stopped looking around. She realized that he'd been doing that for days now, all of them from the ambush had been. Bronwyn looked for Ryland and he was suddenly coming for her.

~~~

Ryland watched her sit quietly in the chair. She'd told him everything that Mike had said to her and now she simply sat there, staring at nothing but the table. He wanted to hold her, but she looked like she'd break if he did. When she stood up he waited for her to pace, but she went to the door instead.

"You said you wanted to run with me. I need that now. Can you…will you come out with me? I don't need sex if you're not in the mood, but I need…Ryland, my cat wants out."

He stood up and started taking off his clothes. When she opened the door and stepped out onto the deck, he followed her just to simply watch her move. Her shift was fluid and without any hesitation. He abandoned his clothes and shifted as well, knowing that he would have to wear tear-away pants around the house if he didn't want to buy suits every week.

She ran for miles seemingly without reason. Ryland saw the other cats and, when they saw him, they moved back. He was glad that she'd told him what they were doing; he'd been ready to have a talk with Mike to find out what he was doing with his mate. Now, he knew the conversation would still happen, but it would be about keeping her safe rather than him backing the fuck off.

When she neared the pond they'd found the first time they had shifted he moved up beside her, but didn't touch her. She drank of the water, moved to the edge, and looked at her reflection. He looked as well, marveling at the beautiful white tiger she'd become.

They're gone, all of them. They always do that when you and I are together. They must trust you to keep me safe. Ryland's cat snorted at her. *I won't leave you.*

Damned right you won't. He moved up behind her and rubbed his body over hers. *You smell good.*

You're marking me again. Are you afraid that one of the other cats will try to move in on your territory? He shook his big head at her. *Then why? Why rub your scent over me out here?*

Because my cat wants to fuck you, love. He wants to mount you from behind and take you to the ground. She shivered, and he could smell her arousal. He growled low in his chest as he moved closer. When she took off he leapt after her, knowing that when he caught her, she was his.

It took him less time than he would have thought to find her scent. When he did, he ran after her quickly, his heart pounding in need. He saw a flash of white just ahead of him and detoured to the left to cut her off. When she crossed just in front of him he jumped out and took her to the ground. His cat growled at her when she tried to fight him. He sank his teeth into her shoulder and forced her to the ground. Christ, he was going to enjoy this.

Don't move. I don't want to hurt you any more than I have to. She growled back at him and he moved over her, still holding her down. She tried to throw him off again and he bit harder until she was still.

His cock lengthened from his body as he moved behind her. Ryland had had sex like this before, but not with Bronwyn. She moved again when he let her go long enough to get a better grip on her. He forced her head all the way down, and she lifted her rear up for him.

He knew that he would hurt her like this. There was no help for it. Were cats were survivalists, and when they entered their own mates, it was to breed. His cock would expand into her and they'd be coupled like that for a while after sex to ensure that his seed was planted.

They'd never talked about children, and he was glad that she wasn't in heat or he'd surely get her pregnant. He moved into her slowly and felt his cock thicken more. She felt it as well, apparently, as she moaned.

You're not supposed to enjoy this. A female cat is supposed to lay still and service her mate. He laughed when she told him she wasn't a normal cat and for him to get to work. *You certainly aren't a normal cat. You're all mine.*

He moved slowly in and out, letting her get used to him. He wanted nothing more than to pound her into the dirt then hold her there until she was in heat so he could fill her belly with their child.

She was rising up to meet his strokes; his balls slapped against her body harder each time. He was as close to coming in her as he could stand when he reached down to mark her. Ryland bit her again, holding his teeth in her until she stopped moving. When she shifted beneath him he felt his balls tighten, his body ready to come. When she cried out her own release he took her hard, fast, and without mercy. Not that she'd beg for it.

His climax moved over him like a soft summer storm. Complete and fulfilling, warm and relaxing, it rolled. He roared as it took him and heard her mewing. Ryland collapsed on her and licked the wounds at her shoulder to make sure there would be no infection.

He lifted his head when she moved. He nipped at her shoulder and told her what was happening. She growled at him.

You could have at least taken me in the soft grass, asshole. There are rocks in places that there shouldn't be. He laughed. *This is so not funny. You're going to dig them out of me when you're finished.*

Gladly. He moved again, trying to take as much pressure off her as he could, and decided to distract her. *How about a baby?*

No, thanks. Having you around is hard enough. I don't want to raise anyone's rug rats that I don't have to. She moved again and he nearly told her she wasn't helping when she looked up at him. *Why do you ask? One of your brothers didn't bring one of the Cunningham kids here, did they? So help me I'll kill them if they did.*

Ryland had met the Cunningham children and could understand her completely. They were evil. He supposed that wasn't the correct term to describe someone's kids, but that was the best word he could come up with for them. He, as well as everyone else who'd come in contact with them, had been glad to see the back of that car when they'd left. And that mother was a piece of work.

I was talking about you and I having a baby. He moved off her and to the ground. He watched her stretch and felt badly for the stones still in her fur. Next time, he'd be a little more considerate. She froze in mid-stretch.

Us have a baby? I don't know anything about them. She shifted, so he did as well. "You can't want me to have a kid. I'll probably leave it somewhere or ruin it. What if I drop it or something?"

"You won't drop it. You'll be a great mom once we tone down the language, and maybe try to have fewer weapons on you when you leave the house. But other than that, you'll be fine." She looked at him like he was being serious. "I was kidding. You'll be a perfect mom no matter if you carry a machine gun on your back and the baby in one of those carriers."

"I wouldn't carry a machine gun with a baby. For one, the gun would be too awkward, and secondly, the baby would be a distraction if I had to shoot someone. Like its father. In his nuts. Shame the kid will be the only one." He lunged for her and tackled her to the ground, careful of where he dropped her. Her laughter made him smile.

"Does that mean you want a baby with me? I would love to see you huge with our child." She smacked him on the shoulder. "You would be a sight to behold."

"Yeah, sure, all five hundred pounds of me." She touched his cheek. "Are you serious?"

"Yes. I want many children with you. As many as you want. All of them little girls with braids and freckles."

"And the people looking for me? What if they find me again? What if Cunningham told them where I am?" He kissed her mouth. "That does not settle anything."

"It does for me." He held her in his arms as he continued. "If someone comes, we'll try reasoning with them. If that doesn't work, we'll sic Mom on them. She's a hell of a lot scarier than you are sometimes. And if that doesn't work, we'll let you deal with them. For good."

CHAPTER 19

The lab was leveled the day after they were married. Sandra wanted them to remain close to her, but knew she was being selfish. She'd been terrified when those men had attacked, and she was still frightened at times in the middle of the night. She was seriously considering Ryland and Bronwyn's offer of her moving in with them. Their house was much bigger than hers and she wouldn't have to do anything. Bronwyn had hired someone to cook and to clean the house. Smiling, Sandra amended that thought...Ryland had hired someone.

It wasn't that Bronwyn couldn't cook, she just hated to do it. Cleaning was something she hated to do when she'd been left in the kitchen. Sandra swore that she'd used every pan, every bowl, and she thought that every piece of silverware had been dirty as well. Ryland hired Mrs. Hopper the next day.

She headed to the post office to get her mail and stopped by the market. The kids would be home in a few days, and she was fixing their favorite meal. She looked up in time to see one of the other tigers, in human form, move to the next aisle. She turned to leave when she felt someone touch her mind.

Hi. She let out a breath she hadn't known she was holding when Bronwyn spoke. *You really should just let me introduce you to them and they wouldn't have to sneak around so you know that they're there.*

Who? That man? You know him? She looked to see if he was still there and he waved at her. *Did he contact you? On your honeymoon?*

No, you did when you became frightened. Besides, we're at the airport now. We decided that we wanted to come home a few days early. Sandra started to ask her why, but Bronwyn spoke again. *Now, go over to that nice man, hold out your hand, and introduce yourself. His name is Carroll. He's there to protect you.*

I don't need anyone to protect me. I have my gun and I'm perfectly fine so long as strange men don't pop out of grocery stores at me. The man came toward her. *He's coming. What do I do?*

Well, don't shoot him.

She might have laughed at Bronwyn if she hadn't been so afraid.

He knows your name, but it would be nice if you told him. Come on, Sandra. I won't give you the gift I bought you if you don't.

That stopped her. *You bought me something? What did you get? I hope you didn't spend a great deal of money. You have to finish putting that lovely house together and—*

Sandra, the man is waiting.

She eyed the older man in front of her. He didn't say anything and he didn't touch her. She wanted to tell Bronwyn that she didn't want this, but she growled at her before she could.

"I'm Sandra Golden. Bronwyn said you're here to protect me. Well, I'm telling you right now that I don't need you."

She heard Bronwyn say, "*oh, brother,*" but ignored her. "And if you think I'm going to have you hanging around me for the rest of my life, you're sillier than she is."

"Hello, Sandy, how are you?"

Sandra closed her eyes to the voice behind her and turned slowly, trying to plaster a smile on her face. Connie Davenport, the woman she disliked more than she did root canals, was speaking to her and Sandra didn't have the patience needed to deal with her today. The woman spoke before she could tell her to fuck off. "There you are. It's been ages since we've had lunch. We should get together sometime."

Bronwyn told her to shoot this woman. Sandra ignored her again, but did smile. She'd said it so gleefully that Sandra found that she wanted to hear her laugh again. She glanced at Carroll and he grinned.

"It's Sandra, not Sandy. I do detest that name. I believe I've said that to you before, Connie." The woman laughed that laugh that grated on her last nerve and had her reaching her hand into her pocket just to make sure, if she needed to, she could shoot this woman. But Carroll touched her arm.

"Mrs. Golden, the car is out front if you're ready to go now. Let me take these up front for you." He moved the cart away and she nearly told him not to leave her. "But I just remembered your appointment at the realtor. If we leave now, we'll have just enough time to get there."

She wanted to kiss him, but only nodded. She turned to Connie and smiled. She was going to take a stand. And this woman had the misfortune of being her first test of the waters.

"I don't really have an appointment. My bodyguard was just trying to help me get away from you. He knows that I don't care for you, as do most people, I would suppose. Not care for you, I mean." She started toward the cart when she turned back. "Also, Connie, if you call me Sandy again, I'm going to shoot you in the foot."

Sandra turned and walked to her cart as Carroll just finished putting the things she'd gotten on the belt. She turned back to look at Connie and nearly laughed out loud when she hadn't moved. Not one inch.

They were putting the last bag in the car when Carroll shut the trunk and took the keys. She glared at him for several seconds before she demanded he give them back.

"Mrs. Golden, as your bodyguard, I should tell you that I don't take orders from you. I will do things for you, help you with your purchases, take out the trash...I'll even massage your feet if you want." He pulled her out of the way of a fast moving cart when it came at her. "But now that I'm someone you know, I will be taking my job of keeping you safe very seriously. My lady is going to murder me slowly and painfully if I don't."

She was in the back seat and he was pulling into traffic when she realized what he'd said. "Bronwyn threatened you? With harm if something happened to me?"

"Yes, ma'am. She said that she protects what she loves. I'm guessing she loves you very much to have you guarded at all times." He swung the car into Ryland and Bronwyn's driveway. Before she could tell him she didn't live there, he was out of the car.

"I'm not staying here. I have a house. Just down the road a ways, but that's where I want to go." He shut the trunk and went into the house. She had no choice but to follow. "I said that I want to—"

She stopped suddenly and looked at the room full of people. They were all there, Ryland and Bronwyn and all her sons. Sindy was there, along with a few people she considered close friends and a few she didn't know. She looked at them through her tears. "I thought you'd forgotten." She looked at the large sign over the fireplace and smiled. "I never dreamed you'd do this for one little old lady's birthday."

Bronwyn kissed her cheek. "It was Alistair's idea. Ryland and I got home last night and hid out in a hotel so you wouldn't know. I didn't think you'd ever go to the grocery store."

"I nearly didn't. I was going to go in the morning and thought the heck with it, just get it over with." She hugged Bronwyn again. "You're the best gift a woman could have."

"You were going to shoot that woman's foot, Mom," Ryland said as he came up to her and kissed her. "I thought Bronwyn was going to wet herself she was laughing so hard. It took her ten minutes to let us know what you said."

She flushed and looked at the girl. "You shouldn't have told them that. Now they'll really have a bodyguard on me."

"You do. Always and forever." Bronwyn kissed her cheek again. "So, do you want your gift now?"

She nearly said something about expense, but it was her birthday and she nodded. Ryland handed her a small box. Nervous and hating to be the center of attention, she tore the paper off. It was a small tube with a sheet of paper under it. When she looked at them, Ryland nodded to the paper. It took her reading it three times before she got it.

"You're pregnant."

Ryland pointed at Bronwyn.

"You're going to have a baby? Really?"

"Yes. In a few more months, but we have to make a deal."

She hugged her before Bronwyn could say anything else. She was going to be a grandmother. A grandmother. "I'll do whatever you want. Anything. Oh, a baby. I'm so excited." Bronwyn looked at Ryland and he grinned. "Well, not anything."

"Too late."

~~~

It was so nice to be home that she walked around looking in each room just to know it was theirs. Bronwyn moved to the second floor to look around, knowing that Ryland would be awhile yet. It was another reason they'd come home earlier than expected. There was a deal that he wanted to try to get completed, and she knew that he wanted it. Besides, she had wanted to come home too.

"We'll have to buy more furniture now. You up for some more shopping?"

Bronwyn leaned back against her husband of three weeks and smiled.

"I know you love to shop."

She didn't and he knew it. But she had some time yet and turned in his arms. Smiling, she reached down, grabbed his cock, and twisted. He held very still. "I'll make you a deal. You can keep this if you do the shopping with your mom about buying the bed and other things in the kid's room." She let him go with a long stroke. "Or you spend the day with me at the gun range and I go with her."

It wasn't much of a tradeoff. She knew he liked the range, and she was getting excited about the baby. Scared, too, about whether or not he'd be normal or not, but she was happy.

"How about if I do both? I would love to go with you to pick out the baby's room. Mom said she has a few things that were ours that she'd like to give you." He kissed her on the nose, something she was beginning to love. "Slick move on your part, making her move in here and use the guards."

She wasn't thrilled about blackmailing the woman, but it was dangerous. They'd not had any more problems, but she wasn't taking any chances…not with any of them. Moving out of the bedroom she'd been exploring when Ryland came up, she went back downstairs with him. She asked him about the deal.

"I'm going to be able to put it together. Mostly because I have the reputation that he's looking for. I want to make love to you in front of the fireplace." She stopped in mid-step on the stairs and looked at him. "I started the fire before coming up to find you. There are two glasses of wine and some cheese and fruit on a platter. Mrs. Hopper left us a nice note telling us that she's gone for the night and that we should enjoy ourselves. I plan to do just that." He picked her up in his arms and carried her the rest of the way down the stairs. When he set her on her feet in front of the fireplace, she looked around the room. He'd been busy.

Dozens of roses were in vases everywhere. There were petals on the floor and the mantle. She saw that in addition to the platter, there were chocolate-dipped strawberries, chocolates, and even some cream. He'd put a soft blanket on the floor, and there was music playing in the background. She looked up at him. "I love you so very much."

He pulled her into his arms and she wrapped her arms around him.

"You might just get lucky because of all this."

"I already did. The day you said yes, you'd stay with me." He started to unbutton her blouse as he continued. "Then you said you'd marry me. And let's not forget the baby."

She stilled his hands with her own. "I'm afraid he'll be like me."

He pulled her blouse down and held it behind her with her arms still tangled in the sleeves. "I don't see why that would bother you. You're a loving, giving person who does more for others than she does for herself. Sure, you have the worst mouth on a person that I've ever heard, but I love you for that too. Any baby you have will have the same personality as you." He laughed. "Okay, now I'm scared."

Ryland finished undressing her slowly. After her blouse, he took off her jeans, moving them down her legs as he kissed a path down them. Her socks he tossed over his shoulder, and then he took one foot at a time into his hands and massaged them until she was moaning. Her bra was next, unclasping the front closure and letting it drift off her arms to the floor. She stood before him in just her panties.

He touched her everywhere, softly, reverently. Every time his hands would skim over her a path of goose bumps followed. She was shivering in need by the time he curled his hands into her panties.

"I've been looking forward to tearing these from you all day. I saw them on the bed when you went in to take a shower this morning and had to jerk off just thinking about them on you. Then I decided to seduce you here, tonight." He ripped them from her body and sat back on his heels to look at her. "Magnificent. And all mine."

Ryland helped her to the floor, touching her more than she thought was necessary, but loving everything about it. She lay before him feeling like a goddess because of the way he looked at her, made her feel. He moved over her, his body settling between her legs as he took her mouth in a gentle kiss. She moaned when he moved his mouth along her throat and then down to her breast. She burned for him, but didn't want him to stop making love to her.

He kissed her shoulder, her arm. Then he moved down her belly, kissing her ribs, then her wrist. He nipped at her waist then her hip. By the time he lifted her leg and rained kisses on her knee and her calf, she was on fire. Still, she didn't stop him or beg him to complete her. Moving back up her body, he kissed her again as he entered her.

Her hands wrapped into his hair and he moved deep into her. Every stroke felt amazing; each time he moved, she wanted more. Feeling him inside of her, having him touch her, she closed her eyes; it was almost too much. When he took her nipple into his mouth, she arched up beneath him and felt him shiver. Knowing that he was doing all this for her made her love him all the more.

"Come for me, love. I want to feel you tighten around me before I have my pleasure."

She came; a gentle yet overwhelming climax took her. As she screamed out her release, her entire body felt it. Her fingers tangled harder into his flesh and hair; her arms gripped him closer to her. Even as he stiffened above her, his body slamming into hers, she came again and again.

Ryland dropped onto her then rolled to his back, taking her with him. She laid over him, her heart pounding and breathing hard. She noticed that his heart wasn't in any better shape than hers. Lifting her head, she looked down at him as he lay there with his eyes closed.

"You're going to have to feed yourself. I think you killed me." She laughed at him and he opened his one eye and looked at her. "Seducing you is much harder work than taking you against the wall. This was more fun and completely satisfying, but hard work."

"Because you couldn't just fuck me, you had to thrill me. I'm glad you did. I needed this more than I can say."

He sat up and put her on his lap.

"You recovered fast."

"Hungry." He fed her cheese and crackers as she gave him strawberries. By midnight, they were making love again. She loved this man more than she could ever imagine.

EPILOGUE

"It says here that there is a DNA test that was inconclusive. What does that mean?"

The man across from Sheldon Pierce shrugged.

"You don't know or you can't figure it out?"

"I figured it out, but I don't know what the hell he was talking about when he wrote it. It says that he created this being. He doesn't call her by any name or, if he did, I haven't found it yet." Tony Brads handed him yet another file. "All I can find is that she was created by him and that he was going to use her for his funding. What funding?"

Sheldon didn't know. This entire mess was brought to him after the man had disappeared some weeks ago. His ex-wife had brought it to their attention, stating that some woman had told her that he had been killed and that she was to go away. She also claimed that the woman had become a tiger. They'd since found that his ex was a major user and liar. Her kids were now in protective custody. And he didn't want to think about those brats.

"I think we should simply put it in a box and forget about it. He was insane, obviously, and his ex-wife? Shit, she needs some serious help."

Sheldon might have agreed on the boxing it up part, but something in the notes intrigued him. Cunningham had created a superhuman by injecting her with other DNA. He thought about what had happened a few nights ago in his backyard.

He had been looking out the window at the coming storm when he'd seen him. There had been a man, then a tiger, then a man again, and he'd moved like he was on speed. Sheldon had gone out to his yard the next morning to find prints, but the rain had been strong and had washed everything away. He looked at Tony when he stood up.

"I'm going home. There is nothing in these files but horseshit. I say lock it up and forget about it."

Sheldon nodded and tossed the file on the desk with the rest of them.

"I'll see you in the morning."

After he left, Sheldon gathered everything he could fit into his briefcase and left too. He had his own printer at home, with which he would make copies of this information that the CIA, where he worked, wouldn't know about. He figured it would take him a week to get it all copied and put back before he put the files in a locked box and forgot about them. Except the ones at his house.

Sheldon wasn't going to give up until he found out if even half of this was true.

ABOUT THE AUTHOR

Kathi Barton, author of the bestselling series Force of Nature, lives in Nashport, Ohio with her husband Paul. In addition to writing full time Kathi likes to spend time with her eight grandkids, three children and three children-in-laws. She writes to relax and have fun.

Her muse, a cross between Jimmy Stewart and Hugh Jackman brings them to life for her readers in a way that has them coming back time and again for more. Her favorite genre is paranormal romance with a great deal of spice. You can visit Kathi on line and drop her an email if you'd like. She loves hearing from her fans. aaronskiss@gmail.com.

Follow Kathi on her blog:

http://kathisbartonauthor.blogspot.com/

www.ingramcontent.com/pod-product-compliance
Lightning Source LLC
Chambersburg PA
CBHW022057170626
46808CB00002B/488